# Praise for

# *BARNSTORMING THE HEARTLAND*

"Wilder's account of his flight in a 1942 Stearman from Maryland to Kansas and back is a lavishly picturesque nine-day travelogue of land and air adventure....articulate and well written.... narrated by a commercial pilot with 20 years of experience selling rides in his biplane to fairgoers ...Wilder's enthusiasm and vivid descriptions are inspiring."

**-*Kirkus Indie***

"As I read this book I laughed out loud with plea-sure, thoroughly delighted to go along for the jour-ney and see the plains of Kansas through Wilder's eyes, smell the Columbian coffee, taste the grease burgers at the local diners, and feel the mist of oil from a leak in the engine. Riding through storms and rainbows, threading power lines, dipping down to read highway signs, soaring over pastures and bays—all of it made me feel like a kid again."

**Amazon/Kindle – "Book Lover"**

# BARNSTORMING
# THE HEARTLAND

*For Don Welsh and John Grace*

*Two great fighter pilots*

*Two great friends*

# ACKNOWLEDGMENTS

Without the help and patience of my family and friends this story would never have been written.

First and foremost, thanks to my friend and soul mate Denise, who encouraged me to take this barnstorming trip back in time to St. Francis, Kansas. She was there when I began to unravel the mystery, and she was there to watch ever so patiently while I stumbled through writing about it.

Also, my undying love and gratitude to my daughters, Jackie and Mel, who were so inspirational and helpful to me with their words of wisdom and journalistic skills. They are the reasons I first recorded the trip, and they kept their faith in me that I would somehow find time to write the story.

A special thank you is due my friend Scott Logan from Arvada, Colorado. I kept talking about the trip so much that he finally convinced me, in his own subtle and diplomatic way, that it was a story that had to be told. Without his encouragement this story would still be locked away somewhere in the back of my memories.

Likewise, thanks to the many friends that responded so positively after I pestered them into reading the manuscript and providing me with the input I needed. Especially, my persuasive friend and editor, Lois Gilbert. I might have given up had she not been there to help. It has been a privilege and an honor to work with her.

And, for the hospitality they have shown to all us wayfaring barnstormers, I will be eternally grateful to the Grace family and the great citizens of St. Francis.

# PART I

## - THE DREAM -

# CHAPTER I

**"IT'S DAWN AGAIN."** Waking up under the left wing of an old open-cockpit biplane, I stick my head out of the sleeping bag just enough to feel the stirring of a morning breeze.

The colors of the sky are subtly changing from pearl gray to light blue as the sun slowly climbs through the golden, wheat-covered Kansas landscape. Soon it will warm my sleeping bag, while Mother Nature ushers in another great day for barnstorming. Heat risers start to lift above the prairie buffalo grass on a gentle south wind. The warm refreshing air lets me know that the hour to greet another glorious flying day is at hand.

Knowing that most people living in the farming communities of the Heartland are early morning risers, the time is quickly approaching for us to fly a dawn patrol around the area in search of our paying customers for the day. However, with the aroma of freshly brewed cowboy coffee on the wind, something tells me my first stop will be the coffeepot inside the Stearman hanger before joining the other fliers in the blue-sky morning.

Squinting out of just one eye to hide the fact that I'm awake, I observe the barnstorming pilot parked next to me. Dressed in his knee-length dark flying boots and brown leather flying jacket, he steps up and down on the left main wheel of his plane while checking the oil level of the big round engine.

Through half-shut eyes I look up and ask, "Is that you, Eric?"

"Yep. I think it's about time to shake everyone out of bed, don't you?"

"Yeah, maybe. Soon as I get my coffee. Man, I don't do anything without my coffee."

For the past ten years I have flown throughout the Heartland with Eric Baldwin, my air show partner and fellow barnstormer. We're both happy to finally be back in Kansas.

While yawning and stretching my arms I add, "It sure would be nice if we made enough money to pay for room and board in a motel for a change."

"Well, you know we're burning daylight," he mumbles as he tightens the oil dipstick back into place.

I reply with a not-so-gentlemanly comment, roll over on the hard-packed prairie grass, and pull the sleeping bag back over my head. I slowly drift into a half-sleep state and begin thinking of home. When I'm on the road with my fellow barnstormers I miss my family, but when I'm home I miss my flying friends on the road. What a dilemma. Regardless of how far away from home I fly, my family is always close to my heart and on my mind. Looking under the right wing I see two other pilots conducting the same early morning oil checking ritual.

The insatiable desire to sleep is interrupted when someone on the right yells "clear" and the pilot swings the big metal prop counterclockwise. Smoke billows from beneath the wings, the engine barks, and a sudden ca-chank, ca-chonk, ca-chank, ca-chonk rhythm fills the air. It's the thunderous sound of a round engine coming to life again. A second engine joins in the symphony and I can feel the vibration through the ground. My stiff and sleepy five-foot-ten body is slowly shaken from the safe and secure cocoon of a well-worn sleeping bag.

The biplane Eric will be flying this morning is a like-new 1927 Alexander Eaglerock. Am I still dreaming about the past or am I actually living the year 1927? If this is 1927, how did I get here? Why have I flown across all those years just to wake up on the hard ground here in this mid-western town? How many more times am I going to ask my family to pay the tremendous personal and financial price they've paid in the past to support this habit of daydreaming and chasing the wind? How many more father-daughter relationships am I willing to risk before I finally wake up and smell the roses? Hopefully my oldest pilot/skydiving daughter will be here over the weekend and we'll be able resolve some of our latest differences. I just hope it's not too late.

"Too damned much thinking before coffee," I mutter to myself as I struggle to pull shoes on without dampening my socks in the heavy dew.

Slipping on my jacket and trying to smooth down my ratted hair, I start the long, 200-foot journey to my morning savior: caffeine.

Walking back to the plane with the promise of chemically induced alertness, I think about all the thousands of miles I have flown and all the miserable weather I have flown through. Once again I have had to accept the fact that barnstormers are indeed a rare breed of pilot. We not only live the lives of gypsies, going from town to town trying to live our dreams and preserve a way of life, but we're also probably one of the least-known groups of professional pilots in general aviation today.

Other men climb mountains; I fly old biplanes. While others are watching TV and its shows on "reality," I lay under the wings of my biplane and watch to the stars dance across an endless cobalt horizon. Right or wrong that's what I do. And once again, I'm back in St Francis, Kansas with the Flying Circus for another weekend of biplane flying and barnstorming. Whether it's 1927 doesn't really matter at this point. This is my choice—or possibly one made for me somehow, long ago—and I gladly accept it as I move on...

# CHAPTER 2

**FOR YEARS AROUND** the second weekend of June, I used to take time off from my job as a Homeland Security planner in Colorado and meet up with some fellow Stearman pilots in St. Francis, Kansas, for their annual Fly-In. It was the highlight of my year: three days of biplane flying, sleeping under the wings, sharing the increasingly dramatic war stories, and just living our barnstorming dreams.

Then, three years ago my dad's cancer resurged and so we moved to Maryland to be with him and the family. I postponed my summer barnstorming trips, but it was a small price to pay for being home with him at the end of his life. It was frustrating to watch him go through unsuccessful radiation treatments that only prolonged his passing. He finally died at home in his own bed, at the age of eighty-three.

I had mixed feelings about him when he was alive, and his death brought a deep regret that we hadn't been closer. I had disappointed him when I left the family business and he never quite understood the wanderlust of my soul. He wasn't a pilot, so he couldn't relate to my desire to fly and my yearning to see what was on the other side of the horizon. No matter the differences of opinion or ways that we chose to live our individual lives, there are times that I miss him very much.

# CHAPTER 3

**I HADN'T PLANNED** to go back to St. Francis last year. We weren't completely settled from our move back to Maryland, so it was a last-minute decision that came without a lot of planning. For the past two years I had been too busy with business and family matters to go. The banner towing and biplane rides I did in Maryland had started in earnest and it promised to be a good season. Once again, I was ready to dismiss the idea for another year.

Then one night in late May a good friend of mine, a fellow Stearman pilot, came to me in a dream. It was the late John Grace from St. Francis, who had died just three years before my dad. John was an Army Air Corps fighter pilot who flew P-38 fighters in the Pacific during WWII. (WWII pilots are my heroes.) He was soft-spoken and slight of build, but his integrity made him a giant among his peers. He usually wore blue jeans, a Grace

Flying Service hat, and prescription sunglasses, and sported a full, short, gray beard. Even in his seventies he still rode a large gray motorcycle all over the country. He started Grace Flying Service after the war and flew Stearman spray planes out of an open field just south of St. Francis. That same field today is known as Cheyenne County Airport.

In my dream I was at the airport talking to some other Stearman pilots. John, a great Stearman pilot and an even better friend, came walking casually by and softly said, "What do you mean you aren't going to St. Francis this year? You promised them that you would come back." And then, just as casually as he came, he walked away.

Waking up shortly thereafter, I thought aloud, "Wow, I guess I do have to go back to Kansas this year." Even after the dream I still wasn't sure exactly why I needed to go. What did it all mean? The dream, the increasing aches in my heart. What should I do?

My wife Denise rolled over, sat up in bed, and asked, "What's wrong, sweetheart? Bad dream?"

"Huh? What? No, just flying in my sleep again," I replied.

"It felt like you were doing slow rolls in the Stearman."

I wasn't sure if it was a good or bad dream, but I knew I didn't want to discuss it in the middle of the night. It could wait till morning. Or at least I thought it could, but I spent the rest of that late morning tossing and turning and wondering.

Over breakfast Denise asked, "Where or what were you flying last night? You kept me awake rolling around and mumbling again."

"It was just another St. Francis barnstorming dream. I was at the airport with some other pilots and John Grace was there. Just the usual flying stuff." I knew I'd need some time to think and digest the dream before talking about it.

"Humph!" she replied with raised eyebrows.

We didn't discuss the dream for a few days, but then one late evening she caught me standing on the west side of the front porch looking off in the distance, daydreaming again. With a cupped hand over my eyes I gazed toward a fading orange ball of sun fire on the horizon. Being so preoccupied, I didn't hear her as she walked up and placed an arm around my shoulder. At first she didn't say a word. We sat down together on the front porch glider to watch the gold shimmering river reach up and slowly consume the last light of day.

Then she firmly asked, "Okay, out with it, what's going on? Is this about St Francis and the dream? You've been awfully quiet these past few days."

"Yeah it's about the dream, but not completely," I said.

I gave her all the details she wanted to know about the dream and then added, "You and I both know I've made some major decisions with less thought, but I'm just having a hard time making up my mind what to do about it."

"Do you really want to go?" she asked.

"Sure, I would give almost anything to go. But who's going to handle the flying business? The biplane rides and banners are just getting started. And I'm in the middle of trying to finish the original paint scheme on that Piper and the buyer is supposed to pick it up by the end of the month. We can't afford for me to be gone for a week or ten days just chasing a dream."

With another lift of the eyebrows she said, "Just a dream? Are you kidding me? John Grace has beckoned you from the grave and you think it's just a dream—I don't think so. Besides, I'm sure the business will take care of itself. You can always call Brian to cover for you for a couple of weeks. What else is bugging you?"

"Do you remember when I drove that car over the side of the mountain on St. Thomas a few years ago? You had asked me not to go on that trip, but I went anyway and had to be airlifted off the islands back to a hospital on the mainland. Well, it's a little bit like that, only different. I have no personal fear about the trip or the plane, but I have a feeling that something significant is in the wind and I'm just not sure what it could be. Does that make any sense?"

She smiled, shrugged her shoulders and said, "Sure it does, but I don't have the same reservations now that I had about that trip. We'll miss you and I always worry about you when you're away from home. But I think it would be good for you to go back to St. Francis this year. And I think you should call and ask Cap'n Don to fly along with you—just in case you get lost."

"Ha, ha, ha," was all I could say. "I can get lost all by myself, thank you very much."

She always seems to know when I need to lighten up. I knew she was right. I just couldn't figure out why I was I having such a hard time deciding.

Actually, the very first person I thought about calling was indeed my friend and flying mentor (Cap'n) Don Welsh from Denver. Over the past ten years we had spent many hours together restoring a 450 Stearman (now my third Stearman), and just as many flying throughout Colorado, Kansas, and Nebraska doing air shows and participating in various Fly-Ins.

Don has always been my special hero. He was a WWII Marine fighter pilot, a retired airline pilot, a great Stearman pilot, and one of the most unselfish human beings I have ever known. He is the one person who had enough patience to teach me a few WWII combat maneuvers and how to do a halfway decent slow roll in a Stearman. When we flew together I always considered myself a student, because I always learned something—either about flying or about life.

# CHAPTER 4

**DURING THE NEXT** two weeks, the sweet, gentle breezes and cool, cloudy days of spring receded, and the long days and warm air of summer moved in. I thought about the dream while suffering from what my family calls "spring flying fever" where my eyes get glazed over and I spend too much time daydreaming about biplane flying, banner towing, spraying, and air shows. While looking west at a brilliant rainbow soon after the passing of a late day storm, the old feelings, now somewhat bittersweet, were pulling at me to once again join my friends. I missed Colorado, I missed Kansas, and I missed flying with my Stearman barnstorming friends. And I missed flying over the heartland with a certain young, beautiful, witty, and stubborn Piper Cub pilot from Kansas City. She can fly the wheel pants off any plane she has ever flown, skydive with the best, and tell raunchy jokes that would make a sailor blush with shame.

But she's too independent, too stubborn, and too damn opinionated, this oldest daughter of mine.

Due to some similarities in nature, we can clash philosophically and retreat from each other for weeks or months. I knew that if we didn't talk soon we ran the risk of destroying our otherwise beautiful father-daughter relationship. It had been about two years since the day we had our worst argument. It was about (what else?) flying and airplanes. At least it started that way.

We had moved her J-3 Piper Cub from Kansas City to Maryland. She was here in Maryland for a visit that late fall day and had just finished flying up and down the rivers around the area to absorb the changing colors. After pushing it back into the hanger she stood for a minute looking at the Cub. She turned to me with a look of both anger and sadness in her eyes and said, "Tell me again why we need to sell the Cub!" She spoke in such a way that I was shocked at first.

I stood there and raised my hands in the air, then shrugged. "It's like I told you kid, the plane just isn't in good condition. It'll cost more to restore it than what it's worth."

"What if we do the work ourselves?" She walked over and started to check out the tie-downs.

"You mean what if Dad does all the work, right?"

"Well, you have restored several other aircraft, including your Stearman, haven't you? I'm sure the Cub isn't that much different."

"Jackie, we've talked about this before." I could feel my anger starting to build.

Through clenched teeth she said, "Well, I think maybe we need to talk about it again."

"As I told you before, I just don't have the time right now to completely rebuild it the way it should be restored. You haven't maintained or upgraded it like you should have, Jackie, and I'd hate to tear it apart and have it sit in the hanger for months or maybe years before we even start on it." I grabbed my jacket and started heading for the door.

"Once again, time for everyone and everything else but me! It's always about you or that damn Stearman." I could hear the crack in her voice.

I turned around and looked at her. "That's bullshit and you know it!"

She was now almost screaming. "No, no, NO! I don't think so. How many family birthdays, anniversaries, and other special occasions have you missed over the years while you've been flying around the country and playing barnstormer? You've never been there when I needed you the most. And how dare you talk to me about what I did to maintain the Cub! You know damned well that I've done the best that I could with time and money!"

Sensing that this was going nowhere, I mustered all the energy that I could to calm down the rage building inside of me. "Okay kid, I don't think this is just about the Cub. Come on, what else is bugging you?"

"All I know is everything has to always be about you or your schedule."

The sadness in her voice made me remember the times she was hurt or frustrated as a little girl. Wanting what she wanted when she wanted it. The way a child can be. Listening to her in this way started to soften me.

"Well, I am who I am and that's the best way I know how to get things done around here, sweetheart."

I started to walk toward her to comfort her. She turned her head around and looked me straight in the eyes with a look that immediately made me stop walking toward her.

"Really? Well now it's MY turn to say that's bullshit. Sell the damn thing; I don't care anymore. This conversation is over for me." She walked to the car. We didn't speak on the way home.

She left later that day for the airport and spoke very little to me before leaving to go back to Kansas City. A hug and kiss for her sister and Denise, but for me it was a look of heartache and rage. Then she walked out the door to her rental car. It broke my heart to see her leave with so many issues still just below the surface. However, I thought that would be best thing for both of us at that time. I had no way of knowing just how long it would be before I would see or talk to her again.

The John Grace dream, memories of the Jackie argument, and the anticipated long trip tortured me for about a week before I finally made up my mind about going. In talking it over with the family

I finally had to agree that there was no way to ignore the dream and what had happened. John had beckoned me from the grave, and I knew I had to answer his call.

So in the last week of May I found myself trying to unplug from everything going on in my world and getting ready for the trip of my life. But I knew there were several obstacles that had to be overcome if I were to leave on time—getting the plane ready for a three-thousand-mile trip, taking care of business, negotiating the weather, and, most importantly, tending to my family. I'd also made up my mind not to leave unless everything felt comfortable and right. And now I find myself first walking around talking to a handheld recorder and then sitting in front of a computer, trying desperately to recapture most of the correct names and details of that trip so that I can share the experience with you. I do hope you enjoy the ride.

I called my friend and fellow banner pilot Brian, and he agreed to tow the banners I had scheduled for the next week or so. I knew I could count on him to handle any additional business until I got back from the trip.

Also, I asked my fellow spray pilot Doug Garey if he would finish painting the Piper for me; he would. They didn't ask where I was going or why I needed some time off. I was glad they didn't. They both knew it's not unusual for me to leave on short notice for a week or two. Also, they were aware that my dad had passed away recently; they probably thought I needed some time alone.

There were several other people, who might like to go along, but something in the back of my mind kept telling me I needed to take this trip by myself; this would not be just another cross-country barnstorming flight. Little did I know it would be the experience of a lifetime.

My fourteen-year-old daughter Melissa (Mel), who likes to hang out the back of her older sister's Piper J3 Cub and take pictures, will probably never forgive me for not taking her along. Well, maybe she will, in about ten or twenty years. She, like her mother, is a hazel-eyed beauty with auburn hair that knows how to get next to Dad with her sad eyes and a drooped lip. But this time she sensed that I would be going alone, regardless of her many attempts to persuade me otherwise. However, I knew we would have to have a talk before leaving.

# CHAPTER 5

**PLANNING FOR THE** trip started with giving my big red 1942 Stearman 450hp biplane a thorough check-up. Like many other Stearman owners, I pride myself on the fact that I keep my plane in almost perfect health and ready to go at all times. However, a second good check on nuts and bolts, a battery charge, and fluid levels is still a must. It's a major effort, but a labor of love.

After owning and flying my first Stearman in Colorado with a 220 horsepower engine, and my second one with 300hp, I decided that what I really needed was one with 450 horses out front, with a big propeller. The performance effect of heat and altitude (known as density altitude) can be a real bear in central Colorado during the summertime. Travel in the mountains is a little hairy without enough power to climb. The Rocky Mountains are very unforgiving to the unwise. Far too many under-powered aircraft have flown into the side of these mountains, piloted by flat-landers who were not paying due respect. I didn't want to add to the statistics.

At first I wasn't absolutely sure that the 450 Stearman I located in Middletown, Delaware, ten years ago was the right one for me. Two WWII pilots that had lovingly flown it only eighty hours in the previous ten years had decided to sell it, but only if they could find the right new owner. Ed Pierce and Bob Bean met me at a small open hanger at the airport to look me over while I looked over the plane. The open environment had caused the paint to fade over the past ten years from bright red to an almost dusty orange on top of the fuse-lage and wings. It was all one dull color without any trim paint. It didn't have wheel pants and the tires were about one-third flat. It had a dirty appearance and it was oil-stained from the top of the right lower wing root all the way down the side to the tail section. I could tell they had tried to wipe it reasonably clean before I arrived, but I knew it had an oil leak somewhere that needed attention. I hoped it wasn't anything serious.

While looking inside the rear cockpit I casually asked, "How much of the background and history do you have on the plane?"

Ed replied, "It had been a sprayer and duster in Alabama for about twenty-five years before we bought it and had it converted back to its stan-dard configuration."

Bob went on to explain. "There were about eighty-five hundred Stearmans built for the WWII

Navy and Army Air Corps flight training effort. After the war they were sold for about five hundred dollars each and the bulk of them turned into crop dusters and acrobatic sport planes."

I added, "I've heard stories from old-timers about buying them for as little as two hundred dollars, when they bought at least five at a time." They both nodded their heads in agreement.

The engine was completely open, without cowling, and had a large air filter mounted on the outside of the left front cockpit panel that looked like a farm tractor filter. It didn't have an electrical system, so it had to be hand-propped to start it. We pulled it out of the hanger and Bob sat in the cockpit at the controls while I slowly pulled the prop around to clear any oil in the bottom cylinders. Then I gave it a couple shots of prime and yelled, "Contact and Brakes!"

He yelled back, "Contact and clear prop!"

It fired up on the first swing of that nine-foot prop.

Bob suggested, "Maybe I should fly around the field with you to point out the idiosyncrasies of this particular 450 Stearman?"

"Hey, whatever works for you tickles me right to death. I appreciate your offer."

I think he just wanted to go for one last ride. I didn't tell him I'd already flown a few hours in a 450. While taxiing out with Bob for a test flight, I noticed a paltry brake on the left gear and a complete lack of brake on the right gear. I thought to myself, *first an oil leak, now no brakes, what next*

*Russ? Have you forgotten that oil leaks can create a fire and that bad brakes can get you killed on takeoff or landing?*

I yelled over the engine noise towards the front cockpit, "Hey Bob, these brakes seem a little weak to me. What's the story?"

"They are, but you get used to it after a while."

I chuckled to myself, shook my head, then responded, "Oh, really?"

"Oh yeah, you need to remember that all the first planes didn't have brakes and most of them usually only had a tail skid on the rear."

I knew that was true about the slower planes of the 1920's, but I also knew that in the 1990's I needed reasonably good brakes on a faster and heavier 450 hp Stearman before flying it to Colorado.

He wanted to make the first takeoff and landing. I agreed to learn from his expertise. He laughed. Bob reminded me that I should take off and land at a little faster speed than normal, to compensate for the weight of the larger engine. He said it would sink and stall a little faster than normal and that I should wheel land it if possible in order to see the runway around the cylinders. I assured him that I was a firm believer in the "tail-low, wheel-landing" technique used by some spray pilots. He chuckled as if to say, "We'll see."

# CHAPTER 6

**WITHOUT BRAKES ON** both front wheels, we had to check the magnetos for rpm drop during a slow takeoff roll. After adding full power, we were airborne in just a few hundred feet and climbing upstairs like a homesick angel. I was really impressed with this performance at almost sea level altitude. Until that day I had only flown a 450hp Stearman from airports at altitudes of three to five thousand feet. I could hardly wait until I had a chance to see how it would perform by myself.

Without radio capability we had to use hand signals in the air to communicate. Bob motioned a flat circling turn to the left with his right hand and I nodded that I understood that he was circling to land. After making a wide circle around the airport he did a smooth wheel landing and then it was my turn.

In order to steer a Stearman on the ground, the pilot has to use both the rudder and a little brake.

First thing I noticed was how wide I had to turn without brakes, but I eventually got turned around and headed into the wind for takeoff. After using a mental cockpit checklist (CIGAR TIP: controls, instruments, gas, altimeter, radio, trim, interior, prop), I started a slow takeoff roll. Also, without brakes, I would again have to check the magnetos for rpm drop while on the roll.

Then after adding full power (2400 rpm and 35 inches manifold pressure), I pushed the stick forward to lift the tail at 40 mph, then started applying backpressure on the stick at 60 mph. We were 200 feet in the air in just seconds, and then climbing on a forty-five-degree angle and indicating 90 mph before finally leveling off at 500 feet. Trimming everything out for level flight, I was soon indicating 125 mph. This was definitely the type of performance I had been looking for, and wanted, in a Stearman. I was so impressed with how it flew that I almost forgot about the oil leaks and the brake problem—almost, but not completely. Poor brakes on takeoff or landing can be disastrous.

After doing a few steep turns over the highway east of the airport, just to get a feel for how it would handle, we came back for the landing. Bob is a big man and sat tall in the cockpit, so I stayed high on final approach, then side-slipped in order to look around him and keep the runway in sight. The front windshield had a film of oil that blurred my forward vision, so I waited until the last fifty feet above the ground to finally kick out of the sideslip and aligned the plane with the runway. Finally the main wheels brushed onto the grass with the tail wheel about a foot off the ground until we gradually slowed down to the end of an almost respectable wheel landing—without brakes. Beginner's luck, I guess.

Bob taxied back to the hanger since he could see the narrow taxi strip better from the front cockpit. At the hanger we got out and he shook my hand and reported to Ed that I was the right person to own the plane.

Then Ed asked, "What do you think about the 450?"

I smiled and said, "Aside from the brake problems and oil leaks it's a real sweetheart." He assured me that these were just minor things.

Bob cautioned me saying, "It might be a sweetheart in the air, but always remember it will chew you up and spit you out and tie your ass in a knot on takeoff and landing faster than the blink of an eye."

I nodded my head as a way of saying that I understood and said, "I've been around Stearmans most of my adult life and have helped rebuild a few after bad takeoffs and landings. So I can appreciate those words of wisdom." We all laughed.

Before leaving I borrowed a jack and removed the right wheel to clean and adjust the brakes. The linings were saturated with brake fluid and should have been replaced, but that would have to wait until later. With folded arms they watched while I worked and occasionally smiled and shook their heads in approval. I think they fully realized that the Stearman N49936 was being entrusted to the right person. Like many other Stearman owners and historians, they knew that you never really own a Stearman, you're just its caretaker for a brief period of time. I tightened several loose clamps on the engine oil lines, cleaned the windshields, wiped the excess oil off the wings, added two quarts, and then took off for Easton, Maryland. I crossed my fingers and hoped everything would keep working and hold together at least long enough for me to get to a good maintenance shop.

# CHAPTER 7

**IT WAS a** late August day with a hazy sun and milky horizon that limited visibility to about two miles. After takeoff I did a low pass over the field at full power and then a fast pull up to five hundred feet and waggled the wings before heading southwest down the Delmarva Peninsula towards Easton airport. Leveling off at about three hundred feet, I noticed that both windshields had already started to accumulate a few oil drops that had been blown back from the engine by the prop.

A few minutes after takeoff I passed over a fork in the road and knew I wanted to follow the next highway to the right, but looking straight ahead into the diffused sun I wasn't sure it was the correct intersection. I decided to follow it for a while and look for the next landmark, a river, on the right. Then a few miles later a light film of oil began to spread over the entire front windshield surface and I missed the landmark. I thought to myself, *Russ, you dumbass, you're lost already.*

I knew I could go back to the airport and start over again, but instead I decided to descend below the trees and, traffic permitting, read the state road signs. After a couple of attempts, I found an open stretch of highway, flew down between the trees, spotted a road sign that read "Chesapeake Bay Bridge 27," and then I knew I was following the right road after all.

Flying alongside Route 301 a couple hundred feet above the trees, I noticed that the tops of all the vegetation appeared more dingy green than their normal fresh green color. At first I thought it was just an early September changing of colors, but then I realized that both of the windshields and my goggles were smeared over with oil. I had tightened several clamps on the oil crossover hoses earlier; maybe there was a crack in one that I missed. The normal sweet smell of oil fumes seemed to be a little heavier than usual, more like burnt oil. *Do I turn back now or keep flying and check it out later at Easton?* Since I was almost at the halfway point of the trip, I decide to stay with the plan and wait.

Later while flying over the small town of Price, I noticed the familiar railroad tracks headed south. I knew that I could follow a path along these through Ruthsburg, Queen Anne, Cordova, and then pass about two miles east of the airport. At that time my forward visibility had been reduced to zilch, since the windshields were completely covered with dark, heavy oil. I pulled the throttle back to 1800 rpm to cut down on oil flow. In order to see around the windshields, I maneuvered the nose of the plane from side to side in a flat sliding motion by pushing right rudder, and then left rudder. That way I could see about a mile straight ahead. I didn't want to run into a tower or another idiot coming the opposite way along the railroad tracks.

At Queen Anne I diverted to the left about half a mile to fly over the in-laws' new farmhouse. Denise was there for a visit and driving up the lane when I dumped over the lines and pulled up along beside her. I did a sharp pull up and then flew a circle to the left and waggled the wings. I could hardly distinguish her through my blurred vision. I wanted to see her smiling face one last time, just in case. She stopped and waved as I flew back west to intersect the railroad on its way to Cordova.

I kept oscillating along with one eye on the tracks and the other one on my finger and map. There was a continuous smell of oil or gas fumes coming into the rear cockpit, but no smoke yet. Every field was starting to look like an alternate place to land, but I couldn't see clearly enough to distinguish trees, fences, or ruts in a landing path. So I pushed on.

Eventually I was able to see the outline of Easton airport about a mile ahead. My goggles and both of the windshields were dripping and completely drenched over with oil. I pulled the throttle back to 1500 rpm. On final approach to landing everything looked hazy and blurry on the ground and there was light smoke and a heavy smell of burnt oil coming from the front cockpit. *Man, you got to get this plane on the ground fast, before it starts flaming.*

After pulling the throttle back to 1300 rpm and tightening my seat belt and shoulder harness, I adjusted the trim and set up for a straight-in landing at 70 mph on Runway 22. Crossing over the approach end of the runway, I had to remove my goggles, stick my head outside the smoking cockpit, and then do another sideslip down to within a few feet of the runway in order to see straight ahead. I leveled the wings with the runway and blindly waited for a three-point contact with the runway. And waited, and waited. Then, as soon as the wheels touched down, the plane started turning first left and then right like a scampering squirrel. Without brakes I pumped the throttle back and forth in order to create a prop wash over the rear control surfaces for some control. That coupled with some fast action on the rudder pedals and I eventually came to a sliding stop at about a forty-five-degree angle to the left side of the runway.

I taxied into the grass beside of the runway, then, after catching my breath, I shut down the engine and walked to the terminal to get a motorized tug for a tow back to a hanger.

But first I had to stop at the men's room. Too much coffee, I guess.

# CHAPTER 8

**UPON FURTHER INSPECTION** in the hangar, I discovered that the oil tank was almost empty. There was a crack in a crossover oil line and the oil cooler was leaking in a solid stream. Before flying on to Denver, I knew I would have to spend another week chasing oil leaks, working on brakes, and trying to rejuvenate the color back to the "Tennessee Red" listed in the logbooks.

After partially cleaning and securing the plane in the hanger, I called Denise to let her know I had landed safely at Easton Airport. I gave a mild version of the oil-streaked flight and told her, "I'm really excited about finally having enough power to fly safely over the mountains when we get back to Denver."

She said, "Let me know how that works out for you." Stearman flying, especially over the mountains, just wasn't her thing.

Most pilots would have never bought this airplane because of its appearance, the oil leaks, and the bad brakes. I was skeptical at first, but from the logbooks I discovered that Sam Wimley from Goshen, New Jersey, had restored it. Sam was one of the finest Stearman restorers in the nation. I talked to him a few months later, just before he died, and he confirmed what I already knew: this plane was a jewel in the rough.

Sam told me, "All round engines leak oil, and sooner or later almost all Stearmans either have or will have a brake problem."

I agreed and suggested, "You have to look beyond these inherent characteristics to find the true heart and soul of the airplane."

After a few years of TLC, a few hundred hours of labor, and a few thousand dollars, this airplane was turned into a top-notch, trophy-winning, Class A Stearman. It still is today.

The plane was equipped with fully functioning dual controls in both cockpits, but had only the basic flying instruments and gauges that it had when it was a WWII trainer. This included a wet compass for navigation, an altimeter, an oil temperature and pressure gauge for the engine, and an airspeed indicator. Consequently, it was certified for flight in clear weather conditions and daytime flying only.

# CHAPTER 9

**TEN YEARS LATER** the only additional equipment I'd added was an older intermittent, handheld, battery-powered GPS, which I used occasionally to pinpoint specific locations for banner towing. Since the plane was still equipped for only clear weather daytime flight, I knew a Kansas barnstorming trip would have to be a seat-of-the-pants VFR flight.

Basically, there are two sets of rules that pilots can follow in the air. These are Visual Flight Rules (VFR), which means flying clear of clouds with three miles of forward visibility, and there are or Instrument Flight Rules (IFR), which means flying in and through the clouds with less than three miles visibility. I had flown Stearmans and other planes on similar trips with less equipment and communication capability, so I felt comfortable planning this basic VFR flight.

With the annual Stearman Fly-In starting in about ten days, I didn't have much time to plan. I was quite busy trying to hand off my banner flying and biplane rides, trying to get the airplane ready, trying to get some rest, and trying to do the necessary survival planning at the same time. At first I felt overwhelmed, but I finally coached myself to just relax and take things one at a time. If everything fell together then I'd leave no later than Wednesday of next week. If it didn't, I wouldn't.

To truly understand barnstorming is to take a trip back in time with a modern day barnstormer; much like the recent trip I took back to Kansas. On such a trip you will feel the wind in your face, smell the smoke off the old round engine, and, if you're really lucky, hear the mysterious singing of the wires somewhere along the trip.

Barnstorming throughout the heartland and across America today really isn't that much different than what it was back in the 1920's and 30's. Flying rules have changed from basic Civil Aeronautics Board (CAB) rules to more stringent Federal Aviation Agency (FAA) regulations. And the aircraft have changed from post WWI biplanes to WWII Stearman biplanes and modern-day Wacos. But the pilot and the dream haven't changed at all. Most every pilot, young and old, has at one time dreamed of taking an old biplane and flying it freely from town to town across mid-America. The fantasy of returning to the early days of flying and experiencing the freedom of barnstorming as a way of life always looms close to their minds and souls.

That dream consumed me most of my life, until so hungry was my desire that eighteen years ago I decided to do something about it. I took the step that would change my pilot's heart to a way of flying, a way of feeling, a way of living: I bought my first Stearman biplane and began an exciting journey back in time.

Almost every year since then I've been very fortunate to spend most of my summers high above the heart of our great nation, barnstorming and selling biplane rides throughout Colorado, Kansas, and Nebraska. Also, off and on for the last few years, I have flown over the East Coast doing biplane rides and towing banners around stadiums and up and down sandy beaches. In a way, biplane flying to me is like drugs to a junkie: I'll take anything I can get. But nothing compares to the freedom of flying in the vast uncontrolled airspace of the Midwest.

# CHAPTER 10

**FOR MOST OF** the next few days I spent working on the Stearman. Denise knew she could find me at the airport wearing oil stained jeans and a khaki shirt or an old flying suit, continuously working and cleaning the old biplane. From experience I knew that, for every hour spent in the air flying this contraption, another three hours of labor would be spent on the ground maintaining the tools of the trade. Moreover, I understand and respect how man and machine are truly dependent on each other for survival in the air and on the ground.

Mel volunteered to help me get the plane ready for the trip. I knew she had something else on her mind so I accepted her offer. Standing inside the hanger with my head inside the engine cowling, I was doing a few last minute adjustments when I heard a soft buzzing. As it grew near I was reminded that I brought her along for the ride and she was busy draining the battery on the golf cart. I heard the buzzing get closer and then a loud screeching noise as she came to a complete stop. At fourteen years old she was still learning how to drive.

"Hey, Dad," she said. "Can I have ten dollars to get some stuff?"

*Not only is she draining the battery, she's draining my wallet,* I thought quietly to myself.

"What kinds of stuff?" I asked.

"Crackers and Dr. Pepper!" she replied matter-of-factly as if I had to ask. We're both addicted to the combination.

"Yeah, I guess so. Just give Dad a second, okay? He's busy trying to do something."

"I know. Whatcha doin'?"

"Well," I began, "see the engine? I'm trying to check it for oil and leaks and to see if things are—"

"Uh-huh. Can I come?" She interrupted my explanation to ask the question I knew was coming sooner or later.

I sighed and braced myself for the "no" I was about to say. This was not any ordinary "no" answer.

"No," I finally said as I wiped oil from my hands and waited for the bite.

We went through a ten-minute plea of why she would be the perfect co-pilot and how she can do it. I really felt bad for her, but I knew she was not up for the unpredictable challenges of flying thirty or forty hours in an open-cockpit Stearman. However, I did listen to her, and I did sympathize with her great attempts to convince me otherwise.

I really wanted for her to go with me, and I felt sad for her because she was trying so hard, but I knew from experience that she didn't have enough flying time to make the trip. When her pouted lip didn't work she decided she would change the subject and try to question me about my world of barnstorming—again.

"Fine, whatever, but why do you fly that old Stearman anyway?"

I thought for a minute, wiped my hands again, then finally sat down with her on the golf cart and said, "Okay, I'll tell you why.

"Since early childhood I've always been possessed with the idea of flying. On many occasions, in my dreams, I would envision myself running across an open field, spreading my arms like wings, lifting my feet behind me and gently rising up over the trees. I would zoom across the fields and towns, seeing it all from a hawk's point of view. I surely must have been an eagle or hawk in a former life, but if not I hope that I will be in the next one. Stearman flying is the best substitute until then."

"Yeah, I know you love to fly, but why a Stearman?"

I scratched my head and thought for another minute then replied, "That's not an easy question to answer, but I'll try again. Before I met my true love, your mother, I fell hopelessly in love with my first Stearman. I was working part-time as ground crew for a crop-dusting company at Easton Airport. At that time I didn't realize it would be a love affair that would last a lifetime. That summer I kept pestering one of the older pilots, Ray Wessells, until I got my first Stearman ride."

"Was it fun?" she asked in wide-eyed anticipation.

"Yes it was, but let me finish my story. Ray said, 'Okay, I'll take you, but you'll have to sit in a yoga position down inside in the three-foot-square dust-hopper, without a seat belt, holding the tank door open.' My immediate reply was, 'Man I can do it; I'm there; I'm ready. Put me in, coach.' I knew that a less than enthusiastic response would mean that he would put me off—again.

He gave me a pair of old goggles to keep the dust out of my eyes and told me, 'You'll have to stay down inside the dust hopper and hold the door open on takeoff and landing. And you need to loop your belt around the crossbar inside.'

'Can do, will do,' I replied, as I strapped on the goggles with a big grin. I helped hand-prop the sprayer to start it, then climbed down inside with my belt in hand, ready to strap myself in. I had to sit in a squatted position since the bottom of the hopper was smaller than the door opening.

After checking me out he said, 'Just remember: you asked for it.' And then he flashed an evil grin."

"Like this?" Mel asked, making her best evil-old-man face.

"Yeah, something like that," I replied. "After doing a ground check, he slowly brought the throttle up to full power, and we headed down a short, narrow grass strip, with wires on one end and trees on the other. Without a seat cushion every small bump in the runway felt like a two-foot pothole, and the noise level inside the tank was almost deafening. I could feel the earth fall away from the wheels as soon as we were airborne, and then a howling rush of wind muffled the other noises. Having the hopper door open created a vacuum that started sucking the residual dust out of the bottom of the tank past my face and I was glad I had worn the goggles. I stuck my head outside above the tank top and held the door open with a vice grip to keep from getting slammed in the head. To my surprise it remained opened on its own. The vacuum force from the open tank held it in place. I looked around, but everything looked blurry and dusty. The wind was buffeting my face and my goggles were covered with enough white insecticide dust to kill every bug in the county.

*So this is what it feels like to be a real cropduster*, I thought. After a while I learned to keep my head facing forward and managed to clear my goggles a little with the back of my hand. I gave a big thumbs-up to Ray, and he thought I wanted something a little more exciting, so he found some electric wires to fly under; but, to my surprise, I discovered that I enjoyed that, too. It was wild and exciting to be so daring and reckless at nineteen years old. And so bulletproof."

I noticed that Mel was starting to get that "deer in the headlights" look, but she quickly refocused and asked, "Then what, then what?!"

That's when I knew I finally had her attention.

"Then, he climbed up higher and did a few loops and some hammerhead stall turns before we headed back to the postage stamp-sized runway. On the way back I could smell the engine smoke and feel the sun on my arms and face. I knew, at that moment, that I would never rest until I could fly a Stearman by myself. I felt like I had moved back in time to a different era of aviation, and I was not anxious to come back right away. By the time we landed I looked like a grinning snowman with a set of raccoon eyes. It was a blast!"

She placed a hand over her mouth to muffle her laughter.

"While working there I earned my first flying hours in a Piper J3 Cub. It was the greatest time of this young farm boy's life. After I soloed the Cub, life was never the same again. A whole new world opened its door to me in the sky that summer. The sheer joy of flying consumed every fiber of my being each time those large wings overcame gravity and lifted us to a different plane of existence. I felt at home with the sky while absorbing the world changing through the open doors of a Cub.

Ferrying spray pilots and chemicals up and down the Delmarva Peninsula and landing in small grass fields and pastures, I found it so incredibly hard to believe that I was actually getting paid for having so much fun. That same summer I learned how to do the tail-low wheel landing used by several Stearman spray pilots and I experienced my

first taste of 12-year-old Kentucky bourbon whis-
key, but not at the same time."

Mel curled up her nose, made a sour face and
said, "Yuck!"

I paused for effect, smiled and then said, "It's
a man thing."

She smiled, and then added another, "Yuck."

"There will always be a special place in my
heart for the J3 Cub, but I knew from day one
that it would be the Stearman biplane that would
eventually consume my heart, mind, and spirit. I
love flying it, but the truth is I live, eat, sleep and
breathe Stearman flying. No other experience
on earth has ever placed me so completely at
one with the sky. And that's why I own and fly a
Stearman.

"Mel, I know you and Jackie enjoy flying in the
Cub, so I have a feeling that you understand what
I'm saying."

"Yes, you both love flying. What I don't
understand is why you and Jackie have to be
so hardheaded that you don't still enjoy flying
together."

I didn't have a simple answer for her, so I shook
my head and said, "I don't know. I just don't
know." I turned away from Mel, headed back into
the hanger, and then mumbled to myself, "God, if
Jackie just wasn't so damn stubborn."

Unfortunately, Mel heard me. She tilted back
her head, looked up at the sky, rolled her eyes,
laughed, and then drove away in the golf cart. I
guessed that our conversation had just ended.

She and Jackie had not always seen eye to eye on many issues either (sibling rivalry, I suppose), yet there she was seeing through both of us so clearly. Talk about wisdom beyond your years.

However, I knew for sure that I had to find a way to go back in time and try to resolve as many issues as possible with Jackie. What I didn't know was when or how. And I wasn't sure I was ready or willing to try at that point. I knew that some of my apprehension about the upcoming trip was about whether Jackie and I would see each other at the Fly-In. And if we did, whether we would be able to turn the clock back on our past.

# CHAPTER 11

**CHECKING EVERYTHING FOR** the third time, I finally declared the Stearman fit for the trip. I threw in the sleeping bag, checked the tool kit and first aid box, added the engine cover and tie-downs, packed some extra oil just in case, then tried to figure out where to put my flight bag. On the floor of the front cockpit, strapped down with bungee cords, was the obvious choice.

Next came the charting. A check on the airport chart supply, at several local airports, told me I would have to buy new Sectional charts as I flew along. I finally called the airport at Frederick, Maryland, and they had the one and only current Cincinnati Sectional chart I still needed. After I explained my dilemma, they assured me they would hold it for me since I would be stopping there for fuel the next week. I also took along a Road Atlas, just in case.

As a spray pilot, most of the fields and pastures we fly into during spraying operations are not on aviation Sectional chart. We use County survey maps and sometimes a Road Atlas for navigation. Little did I know that this practice would follow me, as a backup system, for many hours of off-chart flying.

A long-range check of the weather indicated that we would be under the influence of a large high-pressure area that should hold for the first three days of the trip. The only concern I had was for the high winds and heat that were forecasted for next week as a part of this system. Landing during high crosswinds in a ground-looping Stearman can raise the hair on the back of your neck, possibly make you lose control and wreck your biplane.

With the exception of the GPS, the only time piece in the plane was a 1930s Wittnauer eight-day wind-up clock that I had installed a few years ago. I was told that it wasn't very reliable unless it was wound, "Exactly eight times per day—no more, no less—in order to stay on time." Those were the instructions passed down by a WWI-era pilot who for a short time had been a barnstormer himself in the 1930s. It was the last remaining instrument from a 1929 Travel Air 4000 he had flown in the late '30s and eventually sold in the '40s. Needless to say, I value it more than anything else installed in the plane. Over the years it has become a quirky habit of mine to wind the clock exactly eight times before takeoff.

There was no doubt in my mind that we would slowly move back and forth in time on this trip, but I was still not completely sure how to determine exactly what year it was at any given moment. From the air, rural America still looks basically the same as it did in the late '20s and early '30s. Realizing that time travel was more or less a state of mind, I finally decided to establish the current year by using whatever I observed while on the ground. Seemed logical to me at the time.

While watching some of my previous barnstorming videos again, I waited on the wind forecast to change over the weekend. It slowly became obvious that I would not be leaving on Monday. By Tuesday the surface winds were still coming out of the west, twenty-two to twenty-eight knots, gusting to thirty-four. Wednesday wasn't scheduled to be much better, so I was starting to have my doubts about going at all. But I had promised my St. Francis friends I'd be there by noon Friday, so I decided that Wednesday noon was my deadline for leaving.

Looking over the charts again, I planned to fly straight across Maryland along Route 40, and then turn north to Washington, Pennsylvania. There I would head west, following Interstate 70 to Indianapolis, and then take Highway 36 to St. Francis, Kansas. That was the initial plan.

A few years ago a group of us Stearman pilots—John Schoenhoven (our senior pilot), Jim Walters, Steve Dubois, and myself—were relaxing under the wings of my first Stearman during a typical windy Kansas day in St. Francis. Along with other war stories, John was sharing his philosophy of how "one third of barnstorming is planning, one third is flying the trip, and the final third was talking about it." Since he had flown a Stearman around the perimeter of the U.S. at age seventy, we younger pilots considered his opinion to be gospel. After testing his theory, I added this little planning jewel of advice to my flying bag of tricks.

Experience has taught me to have an overall plan, but to plan only one leg of flight at a time. Too many variables like weather and mechanical problems force changes along the way. You can almost bet the farm on it.

# PART II

## - HEADED WEST -

# CHAPTER 12

## *WEDNESDAY—DAY ONE*

**EARLY WEDNESDAY MORNING,** the air was more hot than warm; unusual for the first week of June. Mother Nature had ushered in another beautiful blue-sky sunrise, with winds less than twenty knots, and the forecast was for calmer winds later in the day. So around nine a.m. it was decision time.

After watching the wind blow for three days, I was at the point where the only thing left to do was strap on the old parachute, step over to the edge of the cliff and jump—or go home.

My pulse rate increased as I tugged the plane out of the hanger, did a pre-flight inspection, and then slowly rotated the prop around by hand to clear any oil in the bottom cylinders. Then, it was time to "Clear prop! I'm outta here."

I climbed up on the wing, then into the cockpit. The starting ritual began: seatbelt fastened, mixture full rich, pump the throttle three times, mixture half rich, master switch on, magneto switch off, yell "Clear Prop," hit the starter button, let the prop rotate five times, then turn magneto switch to both and wait.

A large puff of smoke curled back under the lower wings as the magnetos ignited the primed fuel in the cylinders. After a few low barks, the Pratt and Whitney engine settles into the constant ka-chonk, ka-chank, ka-chonk, ka-chank rhythm associated with round engines. The sweet smell of burning oil permeated the air with a rich aroma. *Houston, we have ignition,* I thought.

Prior to taxiing out for takeoff, I had noticed that some of the hardy sea gulls that usually fly on windy days were huddled alongside the hangers out of the wind. Smart birds. Then I noticed someone in a late model Toyota Tundra pickup truck parked alongside the hangers, as well. He was shaking his head. Probably expressing his disbelief that anyone would even think about flying in that wind. I was almost in agreement.

I wound the eight-day clock exactly eight times and set it for 9:20, while taxiing out for takeoff on Runway 34. Climbing up to one thousand feet out of Cambridge Airport, heading down the Choptank River, bucking headwinds, indicating 100 mph and doing 60 mph ground speed, I knew this would be a long day.

Before heading out across the bay, I flew over Oak Creek on the Miles River to wave goodbye to the family down on the farm. I told them I would fly over if I decided to leave after checking the winds. They weren't home. School was out for the summer and they had gone to town for early morning shopping, probably thinking, "Surely he won't be flying in this wind today."

Crossing the Chesapeake Bay and looking down at the three- to four-foot waves, it was clear the wind gods were still in charge. I usually fly a track across the Bay that would take me from ship to boat for safety sake. But there was only one single sailboat in sight, an eighty-year-old historical Skipjack, and it had most of the sails tied down. The waves were crashing into its hull at about a twenty-degree angle, breaking over the high bow, and then washing across the drenched deck. It made me feel better knowing I wasn't the only foolhardy soul out in a thirty-knot wind that day.

Watching the Skipjack below reminded me of the words inscribed on F. Scott Fitzgerald's tombstone: "So we beat on, boats against the current, borne back ceaselessly into the past."

John Dennis, my first flight instructor, had always instilled in me that "The wind is your boogey-boo." After a few thousand hours of flying I came to realize the wisdom of this statement. Without a healthy respect for Mother Nature, a pilot will soon understand, "There are bold pilots and there are old pilots, but there are no old bold pilots."

# CHAPTER 13

**WHILE PASSING THROUGH** the VFR corridor between Baltimore and Washington, watching controlled airline traffic overhead, I knew who was having the most fun that day. Not having to report to the FAA while passing through this area, I once again realized how lucky I was to be escaping on this flight back in time to an era of less controlled airspace.

After the events of 9/11, the FAA closed this VFR corridor to all civil air traffic unless flying under strict IFR control. A good security move at the time; however, unless the FAA eventually reopens the area to uncontrolled VFR traffic, this gobbled-up airspace will just restrict general aviation further in the long haul.

A check of the old GPS showed I was doing a whopping 55 mph ground speed, and the first leg would take about forty minutes longer than expected. I said to myself, "Well Pilgrim, at this rate you should be able to get there in about a week if you're lucky, barring no additional setbacks." For a moment I had almost forgotten the first golden rule of flying old planes: "If you're in a hurry, take a Greyhound."

Yes, sometimes I do talk to the airplane and myself on long solo flights. I would like to think that I'm not alone in this strange habit. But if not, I doubt that I'll change this ritual anytime soon. It helps me pass the time. I love to fly just for the sheer joy of it all; sometimes not having to talk to the FAA or anyone else only adds to that enjoyment.

As I relaxed a bit and started to get into a GPS navigation mode of comfort, I thought, *Man, having a GPS in this old machine is all right; I can really get used to this.* Content was I to just sit back and enjoy the ride.

It was an older GPS unit with six AA batteries, but it seemed to be right on track most of the time. It had a hookup for a twelve-volt battery, but the plane has a twenty-four-volt system. As a backup, I connected it to a small sealed twelve-volt battery in the baggage compartment area. It was an acceptable setup as long as I remembered to recharge the battery.

The only other small plane I saw that morning was a Beechcraft T-34 about halfway between Annapolis and Frederick. It was Navy blue and had "FLY NAVY" painted on the side. I made a fist in the air with my right hand, pumped my arm up and down twice and said to myself, "Yes! All right! There's another daring soul out braving the elements today. Some people just don't know when to stay on the ground." It was nice to have company.

Descending into Frederick airport I noticed the winds were not quite as strong as they were at two thousand feet. I decided I would try to fly at one thousand feet on the next leg since everything seemed to be going so well. That is if the FBO (fixed base operator) had saved the Cincinnati chart as promised; and they had.

Then, just after touching down on the main gear with the tail wheel about a foot off the pavement, we (me and the plane, that is) shifted sideways from a gust of wind dumping over the foothills. We were headed towards a set of runway lights on the right side of the runway. I thought to myself, *Oh great, not even two hours away from home and you're going to break your plane and bust your ass already. Wake up, amateur!* I had visions of us being spread all over the side of the runway with one wing sticking up in the air and the landing gear broken off. *Get it together, Russ!*

While tapping the left brake intermittently, I pumped the throttle back and forth slightly to blast some prop wash back over the rear control surfaces. Then, with some fast left rudder action we were soon back in the middle of the runway and under control. After slowing down I let the tail wheel settle down to the pavement; pulled the stick all the way back, then slowly applied brakes. Having just been chastised for getting too relaxed on landing, I was firmly reminded that Mother Nature was still in charge.

# CHAPTER 14

**AFTER SECURING THE** plane, a walk-around inspection revealed that all nuts, bolts, fabric, and flying wires were still in place. While cleaning the windshield and wiping down the leading edge clean of bugs, I noticed a few drops of oil on the ramp, but no major leaks. It was just enough to scent-mark the spot, nothing out of the ordinary. *Maybe it's just residual oil drip*, I thought. I checked the tank and added two quarts.

While paying for the fuel and marking my new chart, I noticed a "Class of '93" Navy flying jacket on the back of a chair at the weather computer terminal. It looked brand new, right out of the shipping box. I wondered if it belonged to one of the pilots in the Navy T-34 I had seen earlier. Nobody came to claim it while I was there so I turned it in at the front counter and hoped it would find its right owner. I know how bad I would feel if I lost my A-2 flying jacket.

After returning to the airplane I saw that the usual excited crowd had surrounded my big red 450 Stearman, nicknamed "Le Beast." I found myself enjoying answering the usual questions— How fast does it go?, How old is it?, Is it fun to fly?, Where are you going?, etc. It's always fun and exciting to talk to people about biplane flying and barnstorming. Although sometimes I think I should attach a brochure with FAQ's and answers.

I was able to talk three daring souls into rides at fifty dollars each. Jim and Helen were a husband-and-wife team flying a Beechcraft Bonanza cross-country from Florida to Pennsylvania. They had also stopped in Frederick for fuel. He was a little apprehensive at first, but she really enjoyed her ride. Especially flying low and doing fast pull-ups and sharp turns known as wing-overs.

He seemed content to just talk about avionics, communication systems, and aircraft control centers. I wasn't sure whether he might be with the FAA, so I flew at a legal altitude with the wings unexcitingly level and hoped he enjoyed the city scenery. I offered to let him fly after trimming the airplane to level flight a few miles away from the airport, but he declined.

I enjoyed flying with both of them, but I enjoyed flying with Helen the most. She held onto the controls lightly at my invitation, soaked in the sun and wind, and had the smile and demeanor of a natural biplane flier.

She asked, "Is this all you do, just fly around and sell biplane rides?"

Not wanting to destroy the Barnstormer's mystique, I gave my best Tom Selleck grin and replied, "This is all I ever wanted to do."

"I see, but how far can you go without radios or instruments?" was her next question.

"As far as the wind can take me on two hours of fuel. I'm more of a flier and time traveler than a distance aviator."

I knew that I shouldn't have made such a statement as soon as I said it. One look at her frowned expression through the wing mirror and I already knew that her next response would be "What's the difference?"

Not being sure of her flying background I hoped that I would not offend her with my answer when I told her, "I'm first and foremost a flier, not just an aviator. My chief interest is in flying, not just aviating from point A to point B with all the latest navigation gadgets and communication equipment on the market."

She moved her right hand back and forth across the almost bare instrument panel and smiled.

I paused, but she didn't respond. So I continued, "I fly this old under-equipped biplane just for the sheer joy and love of being in the air with the eagles and the hawks. And I continuously dream about traveling back in time and biplane flying. Flying to me is not just something I enjoy doing; it's a way of life that consumes every fiber of my being to the exclusion of almost everything else."

Looking through the wing mirror I could see that she was smiling and frowning at the same time.

Then, she said, "Have you flown many other types of aircraft or just these old biplanes?"

"Sure, I've flown several different types of airplanes, including ones like your Bonanza, and I've spent over four thousand great hours of my lifetime in the air. However, it's been the nine hundred hours or so of biplane flying and barnstorming that I value the most."

"How long does it take to learn how to fly a Stearman?"

"I'm not really sure, I'm still learning. But what I can tell you is it takes a few hundred hours of flying in one of these old birds before you start to feel like the nuts and bolts of the airframe. Then, when you finally develop that feel of being part of the plane, the sensation of strapping the airplane to your back and flying like an eagle truly becomes reality."

She nodded her head up and down in agreement, but seemed to be deep in thought for the rest of the flight, so I wasn't sure how she felt about my answers until I helped her off the wing. That's when I first noticed that she had a wide smile on her face.

She stepped down off the wing, and then gave me a big hug with her husband standing right there and said, "Nice flying with you Mr. Biplane Pilot. It was really great to go back in time with you."

He looked puzzled, but I knew she would never be the same again. As they walked away, he kept waving his arms in the air and talking at her. She just kept grinning.

The third passenger was my favorite. Sam was a P-40 fighter pilot during WWII and almost had tears in his eyes as he talked and relived his days as a young flying cadet.

I've always enjoyed talking to the WWII pilots who flew the Stearman as a primary trainer. It's so easy for me to fantasize about being there with them and going through the same flying programs. I never grow tired of talking and flying with these heroes of mine, and absorbing their memories and sharing their stories. Stories like when one particular student pilot forgot to fasten his seat belt and fell out of the plane while flying upside down. Or the time when one pilot got lost, ran out of gas in southwest Texas, then spent two days walking back to the military base in Oklahoma.

When I first heard that particular story someone in the crowd had suggested, "Those rattlesnakes grow in number and size every time they hear the story." I laughed and said, "There's no such thing as too many war stories to a Stearman pilot."

Shortly after takeoff I asked Sam, "Would you like to fly it for a while?"

"Sure," he said through a big grin.

His flying style of climbing, turning, and diving (combat evasive maneuvers) reminded me of Don Welsh. I thought to myself, *These WWII fighter pilots all fly the same way.*

He flew most of the time we were in the air, but I took the controls back when we landed. After we shut down the engine he sat and looked at the instrument panel for a while. Then he finally stepped down off the plane and said, "That was a great ride, how much do I owe you?"

I replied, "It was an honor and a pleasure flying with you, Sam, and I really enjoyed hearing about your adventures. How about forty bucks to cover the expenses?" He gave me a fifty-dollar bill that I tried unsuccessfully not to accept. He said the memories were worth a lot more.

# CHAPTER 15

**I PROBABLY COULD** have hustled up a few more rides, but I needed to stay on schedule, so it was time to clear prop and head for Washington County, Pennsylvania. While taxiing out for take-off, the 1993 Navy jacket was still on my mind and I made a wish that it would safely find its owner.

While giving those three rides at Frederick airport, and again on departure around midday, I noticed the gusty wind had started to pick up again. After leveling at one thousand feet, I found it too rough to enjoy so I eased on up to fifteen hundred where the wind was stronger but a little more tolerable.

I could hardly believe that I'd made one hundred fifty dollars in rides already. "Hey, maybe I'll be able to stay in a motel tonight and have steak and eggs for breakfast in the morning." But I knew that most of the money would probably be spent on fuel getting Le Beast to St. Francis; unless I got a few more rides.

Cruising along over the rolling hills of western Maryland was scenic and peaceful. The warm sun was starting to take effect as I bumped along over the waving peaks and valleys trying to enjoy the landscape. I had become very comfortable with my new GPS mode of navigation.

Even my 55 mph ground speed was starting to become more acceptable. We were at least keeping up with the cars on the highway below; hadn't been able to do that earlier along the interstate. Approximately halfway to Washington County, I noticed the fuel gauge was down to less than half a tank so I diverted to Cumberland, Maryland, to refuel and take a lunch break.

After landing and taxiing to the terminal for fuel at Cumberland, I began to notice the improvements made over the past decade. I had landed here for fuel about ten years ago only to discover a large fuel truck, but no fuel. At that time Jim Walters and I were flying this newly purchased Stearman to its new home in Denver. Not having enough fuel to go farther, we had to go down the hill and purchase gas cans and fuel to fly on to Bedford, PA. It was a good thing the 450 Pratt and Whitney engine could burn auto gas.

I parked north of the terminal and began a "look over" of the plane. That's when I discovered that the oil drips I'd seen at Frederick Airport had turned into an oil slick reaching almost the length of the fuselage. Checking the oil level, I found I had lost about a gallon in just over an hour. This was definitely an "Oh Shit!" situation. A few years ago an oil cooler leak had grounded me for two days on a similar trip.

Having just been tossed around in this old bucket of bolts, flying wood and fabric for almost four hours, this was the last thing I wanted to see. It had to be approaching at least ninety degrees by that time. To say that my patience level was at its best would have been like saying it's mildly warm in Phoenix during the summer months.

I said, "Oh man, I've got a bad oil leak and I'm going to get stuck here. It's probably that damn oil cooler that's screwing up again or something worse."

I kicked the right front tire and hurt my toe, so I hit the prop blade with the base of my fist and hurt my hand. Both gestures did little to improve my mood. I limped away slowly, mumbling obscenities galore.

I hoped someone would steal it while I was inside so I could collect the insurance and buy a real airplane—maybe one with all the latest in avionics and an engine that didn't leak oil.

# CHAPTER 16

**ALL OF THESE** emotions and problems were coming to me well past lunchtime. I decided to grab a bite to eat and think about it. After sitting in the air-conditioned restaurant with a nice club sandwich, some cold iced tea (and flirting with a really cute waitress), things didn't seem quite as overwhelming. I think it was the iced tea that did it.

After I got on a first name basis with Susan, the waitress, she asked, "Where you headed?"

With a determined look I replied, "I'm headed to St. Francis, Kansas, for our annual Fly-In."

"What's in St. Francis?"

"Hopefully, some generous barnstorming customers."

I knew the next question before she even asked.

"What's barnstorming?"

I asked, "Are you sure you really want to know?"

"Sure, why not?"

"Okay, but remember you asked, and I just might have to shoot you if I share any 'Top Secret' information."

We both laughed and I began my sales pitch: "Barnstorming is one of the oldest professions in aviation that only a handful of pilots have ever truly experienced as a way of life. In the 1920s and '30s, the fliers tried to make a living by flying old biplanes around the country and selling rides to anyone who was daring enough to give it a try. That's the short version of a barnstormer's life."

With a quizzical look she thought for a second or two, then smiled and said, "Cool!"

It was extremely rewarding to know that I was still "Cool!"

With that type of encouragement and a few more glasses of iced tea, I shared a few war stories about barnstorming, biplanes, and St. Francis, until her eyes started to get that glazed over "deer in the headlights" look.

Realizing she was probably saturated with flying, I asked her about the gold "1986" pin on her lapel. She shared a story about her high school reunion and how her classmates looked so different after just a few years. Then she talked and talked about what everyone was wearing and what everyone was doing with his or her lives, etc. It wasn't long before I started to get that same "deer in the headlights" look myself.

However, I had managed to get my mind away from the airplane and started thinking about the first barnstormers who flew these old biplanes, and some of the stories of their misadventures. They, too, had to deal with whatever fate dealt them on a daily basis, patch it up with bailing wire or tape, and then just keep going. Most of the time you are completely on your own when something happens to one of these antiques. Very few maintenance shops will even look at a wood and fabric airplane, and radial engine mechanics are almost as scarce as a Democrat at a GOP Convention.

After lunch I went out to inspect the airplane again. What at first appeared to be a major oil leak turned out to be a cracked fitting on the oil cooler and a hose clamp that needed to be replaced. As expected, the maintenance shop at the airport didn't have any parts for a fifty-year-old engine. I borrowed the courtesy car and after two hours of running around Cumberland I eventually found a satisfactory substitute fitting in a local hardware store. Aside from the mess, there was nothing really too severe about the repair after all. After about two hours of sweat and profane work, I once again wiped down the fuselage and wings.

At first I had been a little discouraged; however, I knew that it's just one of those things you have to live with when you own or fly one of these old biplanes. After each flight it should be second nature to look it over to determine if everything is staying tight and glued together, just to be sure you haven't ruptured a hose or broken something.

On pre-flight I walked around the airplane and talked to it gently, saying something like, "You raggedy-ass old airplane, I'll kick your damn tail feathers off right now unless you straighten up your act. I'll leave your temperamental butt out here somewhere in the mountains and catch a donkey ride back home." Getting no immediate feedback, I assumed this was an acceptable agreement, but I still planned to keep a cautious eye on this unpredictable machine.

Susan the waitress decided not to take the ride I offered her before departing. Must have been something I said about "that lousy old bucket of bolts" while drinking the iced tea.

It was time to clear prop, I'm outta here. I automatically rewound the eight-day clock eight times and taxied out for takeoff again.

# CHAPTER 17

**WE FLEW THROUGH** "The Narrows" a few miles west of Cumberland. This famous one-thousand-foot-wide gap in Wills Mountain was originally known as "the Gateway of the West," since it provided a convenient road westward. Flying through the pass was not only awe-inspiring, it was breathtaking. But going through there with minimum instruments when it's overcast is a hair-raiser. The terrain starts to run uphill and it's sometimes hard to distinguish the horizon from haze.

Ten years earlier, Jim Walters and I had turned around abruptly over Frostburg College while trying to clear the mountain tops there. We had to fly north and then back west through an overcast valley in Pennsylvania just to get through that early September haze.

Today, on this clear windy day in June, the visibility had to be at least twenty or thirty miles. Checking the wind and the chart again after takeoff, and then reviewing the next leg to Washington County Airport in Pennsylvania, I thought, *Hmm, this GPS works so great I think I'll just cut right across West Virginia instead. Won't even stop at Washington County Airport. I'll go right through West Virginia then across Ohio and I'll save myself some flying time, especially since I got held back with that wind.*

So I did. Cutting across West Virginia instead of going north to I-70 and cruising along across the beautiful lush green mountains I thought, *Oh man this is cool. I wish Jackie were here to share all this with me. I bet she would've got a kick out seeing me lose my cool and kicking that tire earlier.* A few minutes passed and I looked at the GPS again. It was staying on the same miles per hour, and on the same heading, and I thought, *Hey, I'm even better than I thought I was.*

After a while I checked it again only to discover my distance, heading, and ground speed were staying the same. Then, after pushing the refresh function, it still had the same indications it had given about ten minutes earlier. A second and third attempt didn't change its mind either.

The damn thing had just locked up on me, cold turkey!

Looking down at the jagged West Virginia Mountains I thought to myself, *Not only does it not know where it is, YOU don't know where the hell you are either, smart ass.* Looking in all directions, there was nothing to see but green mountains without distinction. Reluctantly, I did a tight, climbing, one-hundred-eighty-degree turn; kept my finger on the chart; finally found a road that led to a city; then figured out where we were, exactly. I was very happy to be flying blue sky VFR.

It just so happens that I did have my chart under my right leg and I had drawn that line across West Virginia as an alternate route. It was at this point of the trip I decided to once again stick my finger back on the chart and it would stay there for the rest of this trip. I decided then and there that I wasn't going to trust the GPS again anytime between then and when I got back.

After backtracking a ways, then heading north, I decided to stop at Washington County Airport after all. We arrived with plenty of fuel and it felt good to be back on track. But I relearned a lesson: "Don't stick your neck out on a single radio, because somewhere along the line you might get your head chopped off."

Pilots can use all the satellite navigation equipment they want, and they can worship all the instruments and radios they desire, but they should also know where they are on the map all the time. It just might keep them from busting their ass or getting into a tight spot.

Its Murphy's Law: if something is going to stop on you, it's going to stop on you when you least expect it. And that could very well be out over the mountains or the middle of the ocean.

# CHAPTER 18

**THE FOLKS AT** Washington County Airport are very congenial hosts. Steve Dubois, my spray pilot friend from Colorado who flew this Stearman back to Maryland for me three years ago in a November snowstorm, had stopped here on his trip. They let him hanger the plane here while he and his passenger stayed overnight in town. He still talks about how pleasantly he was treated.

Once again they offered to let me keep the plane there overnight, but I had already decided that I wanted to make it as far as Indiana before stopping for the day. I thanked them for the offer, filled up with gas, cleaned up a bit, then walked around the plane and reflected on that damn GPS.

I wasn't just frustrated; I was getting hot, tired and pissed. I mumbled, "You son of a bitch, I outta rip you out of there right now and throw you down on the ground and stomp up and down on your ass a dozen or so times." However, I realized I wasn't wearing the right shoes to hand down the justice it truly deserved. Also, I didn't want to embarrass myself in front of potential customers (or hurt my sore toe).

In talking it over with another pilot at the airport, he calmly suggested, "Well, maybe it just lost itself; sometimes they do that."

Somewhat embarrassed, I replied, "I remember doing a cursory location check when I left home, but not a full position fix."

Then I remembered that it takes about forty minutes, outside the hanger, to reprogram a complete relocation fix on this older unit. After ten seconds of further contemplation, I decided to wait until I got to St. Francis to deal with it.

This was the second time it had locked up on me, and I wasn't too sure I'd ever trust it again anyway. The last time it had locked up was when I was flying an "IMPEACH CLINTON" banner over the Delmarva Peninsula and up and down the beaches.

On preflight I was overjoyed to find no new oil leaks. Shortly after the GPS situation, I had been in the frame of mind to call the trip off if it was still leaking. Thought I might stop right there, spend the night and fix whatever needed to be fixed, then wait till next year. Then, I remembered Jackie, John Grace, and the dream. I knew I had to keep going.

Suddenly, I realized that I had almost one fourth of the trip behind me; I started getting excited again. Sometimes a little venting of anger or a rush of adrenaline helps clear the mind. I was starting to feel good; so, "Clear Prop! Indiana, here I come."

I started to wind the eight-day clock again, but it suddenly occurred to me that there had been no obvious time change on this leg of flight. If anything we had moved ahead a few years.

The most noteworthy observation was a 1990 edition "Trade-A-Plane" periodical in the corner of the workshop I spotted while talking to the pilot about the GPS problem. Either it was 1990, or maybe time stands still in this part of Pennsylvania. Or maybe I had over-wound the clock. Yes, yes, that's it! I had rewound the clock in Cumberland for the second time today. The WWI barnstormer pilot had said, "Wind it eight times per day," not every two hours, you bonehead.

I decided not to wind the clock any more that day.

# CHAPTER 19

**WASHINGTON COUNTY AIRPORT** is just south of Interstate 70 so I decided to remain a few miles south, but somewhat within visual distance of the highway, at least until I got to Indianapolis.

Having made the decision to not use the GPS for the rest of the trip, I re-marked my chart in twenty-mile increments for the next leg. I knew I could fly at least two hours (about two hundred miles) before having to land for fuel. Ground speed was no longer a major factor, just time.

It wasn't long before we were back over the mountains of Pennsylvania and headed for Wheeling, West Virginia. The valleys and small fields were awash with a flood of colorful maples and apple trees. It was hard not to notice these deciduous trees slowly give way to the heartier darker pines and cedars as we slowly climbed in altitude to clear the mountain ranges.

Drifting lazily along with my finger back on the map and my head out of the cockpit watching for landmarks, I could hear the wind faintly singing in the wires for just a brief moment. I began enjoying the trip anew as I breathed in the beauty of western Pennsylvania and crossed into northern West Virginia. Flying in an old open-cockpit biplane is a breathtaking, almost spiritual experience if you just relax and let it happen.

Le Beast and I were friends again—at least for the moment.

While flying along a few hundred feet above the rolling hills I noticed an open field of tents on one of the peaks. Circling a little lower I realized it was a Boy Scout Camp. A large group was in an open field heavily engaged in some type of game or sport and kicking up a lot of dust.

Descending, with a three-hundred-sixty-degree turn with the smoker on, I brought most of the activity to a halt. I pushed the throttle back and forth a few times to make it sound like I was having engine trouble. I grinned as I flew down through a valley below the tree level and out of sight, and then continued on my way.

They were probably disappointed in not seeing the crash. I always wondered if they sent out a search party looking for my remains. Some of my fondest memories of childhood included watching airplanes overhead; maybe some young fledgling wannabe pilot might have been doing the same today. I hoped so.

# CHAPTER 20

**SHORTLY THEREAFTER, THE** foothills of Pennsylvania and West Virginia slid beneath my lower wings, and I crossed over into Ohio and headed for Columbus. Looking at the chart, I knew I'd have to divert a little south to remain clear of the controlled airspace around the airport. So far I had not used the handheld radio or talked to anyone on the ground—but I continued to monitor all the right frequencies, just in case.

Having flown about six hours, I was starting to wear down a bit. By late afternoon the wind and the sun were still strong on the nose and the air was still hot. I hoped it all would decrease over the flatlands so that I could reach Richmond, Indiana, without having to make another fuel stop.

If necessary I planned to stop in Zanesville, Ohio, where I had stopped for fuel ten years earlier on my way to Denver. By the time I reached Zanesville, I estimated that I would make it to

Richmond with a few gallons of petrol to spare, unless the wind gods decided otherwise. So I kept going.

It was just a hop, skip, and jump on out to Dayton, where I would again have to fly south around the airport airspace. Looking at the chart, I suddenly realized how close I was to the historically significant Wright Brothers hometown. I had wanted to stop and have a look around, but I needed to get to Richmond before dark.

I will never be able to fly or drive across Ohio without thinking of the Wright brothers and their contribution to aviation. Who would have thought that two bicycle mechanics could have given so much to the world? Wish I could have been there at the beginning to witness their early flying feats.

Actually, I think I'm able to appreciate their accomplishments more now than I would have then. If only they could see the aviation and space programs today. It didn't surprise me when the reenactment of their first flight at Kitty Hawk in 2003, by the Experimental Aircraft Association (EAA), was unsuccessful. I think that even today we take flying for granted and still cannot fully appreciate their ultimate contributions.

What the EAA needed at Kitty Hawk was a good Stearman pilot to fly the Wright replica biplane. Preferably one with experience flying slow, underpowered, and heavily-loaded spray planes on the edge of stalling at all times. But, hey, nobody asked me.

Crossing the Indiana state line, I gradually descended south towards the Richmond airport. Turning back west towards the hazy setting sun, we slowly sank below its golden glow of the day. It was the right time to stop for the day.

While taxiing to the terminal, I noticed another Stearman parked out front. It was painted in a yellow Navy scheme with a 450 engine hanging on the front. I thought, *All riiiight, this is great. There must be another Stearman pilot around here.* I get newly excited every time I see one of these old birds. I really got worked up when I discovered there were two 450 Stearmans based here. Time permitting, I hoped to meet both pilots and maybe swap a few war stories.

I asked the guys at the FBO about getting the airplane inside for the night. They said, "Sure, you can put it over in the jumper hanger."

# CHAPTER 21

**AFTER TAXIING OVER** to the hangar and shutting down, I found myself surrounded by several wide-eyed skydivers asking about the possibility of my being around for the weekend. Seems they were having a "big boogie" over the weekend, and, like most skydivers (including Jackie), they wanted to jump from a biplane at least once in their lifetime.

Unfortunately, I had to tell them I was running late to be in St. Francis by Friday, but I did agree to do a few jumps early the next morning before leaving. Three of them said they would take me up on the offer and helped me push the plane inside. I appreciated their help; I was one tired puppy with seven hours of flying time weighing on my tail. I noticed their bright colored jump suits were flared out like the bell-bottom pants of the 1970s. *Is this just style, or am I slowly moving back in time again,* I wondered.

I was ready to call it a day. It was a good day overall; I'd had a few problems, but nothing major. It was good to be back barnstorming again. It felt good to be talking to people about the plane and seeing them get excited about taking rides.

After cleaning the plane, I took the courtesy car into Richmond and checked into a local cheap motel. The restaurant next door had a tolerable evening menu and good decaf coffee, so I asked about breakfast hours and found that they opened at six a.m. sharp.

Mel was still disappointed about the trip when I called home around nine p.m. I could almost see the drooped lip. She was still in the denial stage; how I could possibly leave without her? I told her I really missed her and I wasn't having any fun yet, but I was still trying. She said, "Yeah, I'll bet you're not."

I gave them the fast and up-side of the trip so far. They talked and talked about the infinite details of a good shopping day at the thrift and antique stores. It was so good to hear their voices. I listened and listened. If possible, we always talk at the end of the day when I'm traveling.

I was looking forward to getting a good night's sleep and doing a few jump rides in the morning, and then maybe making it as far as Concordia, Kansas by day's end tomorrow. I was tired, but still excited about rejoining the other Stearman pilots at the Fly-In on Friday for three days of barnstorming, relaxing, and swapping war stories. It would be great to see everyone again.

I wondered if Jackie might possibly fly up from Kansas, and I thought about who else would show up in St. Francis over the weekend. Would Eric be there with several female followers, like in the past, or had he just brought one special guest for the weekend? Had Jim Walters finally finished restoring that 450 Special he'd been working on for eight years? Would Don Welsh be there to give me some more pointers on my acrobatic routine? What new stories would John Schoenhoven have to share with all his junior pilots, and how many pilots would be sleeping under the wings that year? I hoped Steve Dubois would show up in his new Stearman, with or without his tent. And would Doc Kimball bring both the T-28 and the Stearman to the Fly-In? After two years it would be great to share a few beers at the local watering hole and get caught up on each other's lives.

# CHAPTER 22

## *THURSDAY—DAY TWO*

**TRYING TO WAKE UP** my mind, body, and spirit on the second day—over numerous cups of coffee and steak and eggs—I headed back out to the Richmond airport early enough to take the skydivers up for a jump. On the way to the airport the winds were already starting to blow again so it was doubtful that the jumpers would show up for a ride. They didn't; it was a wise decision. Jumping in too much wind can be a hairy exercise at least, and a near-death experience at most. No need to tempt fate.

The airport staff showed up around eight a.m. I offered to fix the coffee after I saw a large can of Colombian on the shelf below the Mr. Coffee maker. They agreed.

"Has anyone checked the wind and weather forecast?" I asked as I spooned in several over-filled scoops of Juan Valdez.

Their answer was, "Surprise, surprise, it's still the same: 'clear, hot, and windy' for the rest of the day."

I was beginning to think I was already in Kansas.

While taxiing out for takeoff with a good caffeine buzz, I reached forward to wind the clock eight times, but then hesitated for a minute. I thought, *are you really going to believe that going forward or backward in time can be controlled by how many times you wind that clock? What an imagination!* At that point I wasn't sure, but I decided to wind it just 8 times for the entire day and see what happened.

By eight-thirty we were working our way back north towards the interstate and heading towards Indianapolis. I noticed that Le Beast was climbing unusually fast today, the damp and cool morning air refreshing both of us. We were above four thousand feet and still climbing. A check on the chart showed we would have to be above forty-eight hundred feet to fly over the control area around the Indianapolis airport so we continued climbing and then leveled off at fifty-five hundred feet.

Crossing over Indianapolis, I caught sight of the Speedway just as it passed my right elevator and I thought, *Oh man, we just missed it.* Not to be deterred, I pulled the nose up, pulled back the throttle, then rolled over into a slow, inverted, diving one-hundred-eighty-degree turn and was able to see it fine. It felt so good I did it again before heading back west. I had wanted to do a slow roll over the Speedway, but I had too many loose items inside the cockpit and baggage compartment. Maybe next time.

Doing the first time check, I noticed I wasn't making too much headway at that altitude, so I pushed the nose over and headed back closer to terra firma. Another reason the airplane was climbing so well was the upper headwind; the surface winds would be slower, but rougher.

# CHAPTER 23

**NORTH OF TERRA HAUTE,** Indiana, and realizing my ground speed overall was a bit slower than expected, I began thinking that maybe I should stop for fuel earlier than planned. A refueling stop at Tuscola airport along Highway 36 was planned, but at that speed I was starting to wonder about making it that far.

I lost a considerable amount of time climbing over the controlled airspace around Indianapolis and staying above two thousand feet along the way. *Next time I'll stay lower and fly under the airspace,* I thought. I decided to keep going and fly a little lower and slower for the rest of this leg to save fuel. Unless the headwinds increased, we should make it okay.

I always plan for a maximum of two hours of flight, plus ten minutes for takeoff and landing. At one hour and fifty minutes into this leg of the flight, I knew I could fly maybe another twenty minutes max before running out of fuel. Highway 36 started looking like a great alternate airport by this time.

A few years earlier I had successfully landed a fully loaded fuel-starved spray plane on a county road in Colorado. That particular day I was in a hurry and had let someone else refuel the plane while making a pit stop. In my haste I forgot to double-check the fuel caps. Because of a cocked fuel tank lid, the lift on the upper wing had siphoned most of the fuel straight up and out of the tank by the time I arrived back at the spraying field. I didn't want to repeat that landing experience in a Stearman.

I rechecked the chart and my road atlas for a closer airport. With none available, I reduced the power settings even more to conserve fuel, I crossed my fingers, and kept going.

My next time check told me what I didn't want to know. The wind gods were still against me. Somewhere in the back of my mind I heard the faint voice of my first flight instructor saying, "The wind is your boogey-boo." I had just passed the two-hour point of the flight, but I remained confident that I could somehow make it to Tuscola airport—even though the "seat cushion pucker factor" had increased exponentially. Since the fuel gauge had almost quit bouncing off empty, I knew it would be only ten to fifteen minutes before that windmill out front stopped churning air. I pulled the throttle back a little more to stretch the distance.

Easing the plane over the top of the power lines and lining up with the highway I discovered that, should the engine quit, the distance between the poles was too close for a landing on the roadway. The fields along this particular stretch were too rough or had too many fences and trees to permit any type of landing without busting my ass and wrecking the plane. Looking north and south, the landscape appeared the same. In each direction all I could see was small fields, chunks of rock, groups of trees, and unfriendly terrain with no safe place to land. Only one thing could happen: both man and machine would be destroyed this day. Envisioning all the piles of Stearman wreckage somewhere down in one of those fields, I knew along with the rubble would be a tombstone that read, "This is where Russ 'Dumb Ass' Wilder ran out of gas."

Thoughts of meeting my maker flooded my mind and I was ready to humbly submit to my fate. I was beginning to compile all the promises that could be made just to spare me from death for another day. I could promise to give up smoking, drinking, and wild women, but then I realized I wasn't doing any of that; aside from barnstorming, my only vice was an occasional beer or two. I didn't think my sins were great enough for bargaining, so I checked the map again and realized that I was still at least ten miles from the airport. On the map, and in my mind's eye, the distance was starting to look more like one hundred miles.

I eased the plane over the trees and flew closer to the ground hoping to ease its weight through the lift provided by ground effect, which is heat rising off a hot surface. At that point I was willing to try anything to lighten the load.

All those years of flying were coming to a close there on the stone-ridden fields of Illinois, and all I could do was wait. I had wanted desperately to head north or south to search for one of the private airports listed, or at least to find a better crash site, but my fixation on Tuscola and all those years of flight training told me to "Stay with the plan." So I did.

I tried moving the stick back and forth in short jabs to see if I had enough fuel in the tanks to move the gauge, but nothing happened. Then I tried kicking the rudder pedals right and left to jolt any fuel that might give me any hope. Still the fuel gauge didn't move. The thunderous roar of the engine began to fade as my heartbeat grew faster. My ears were starting to ring and my breathing rate increased. I could almost hear the engine slowing down, but the tachometer was still indicating 1800 rpm. I slowly pulled it back to 1700, hoping to stretch the distance. I hoped the winds would subside just long enough for us to reach the airport.

I started talking to Le Beast. "Come on, sweetheart. Come on, baby. Just a few more miles. Forgive me, my friend, I should have known better. If this is it, I hope we both come back as eagles." Ironically, I found myself hoping that enough of the plane would survive for someone else to restore later.

While starting a gradual climb to get more altitude for better visibility, I tightened my seat belt and shoulder harness to increase my chances of survival. I went through a mental checklist for emergency landing and waited. And prayed. The Great Spirit had pulled my miserable undeserving bacon from the fire on many occasions in the past; my only prayer was that She would be listening again on that day.

I squinted my eyes to see something on the horizon through the oil spots on the windshield. As I got closer I realized it was an older VW bus crossing the county road ahead. I thought aloud, "Maybe I can land on that road if there are no power lines." But as I flew closer in I saw that the road was lined with phone wires on one side and electric wires on the other. I just couldn't win.

Then, just when I was ready to accept my demise, I looked beyond the crossroad and saw that beautiful Tuscola runway slowly rising up from the airport surface, about five miles ahead on the nose. With no traffic in sight I set up to make a straight in approach and started holding my breath. As the plane crossed the runway threshold I grinned and said to myself, "No sweat, Russ," and the seat cushion slowly returned to its normal position.

# CHAPTER 24

**AFTER LANDING AND** paying proper homage to the wind gods, I started taxiing back south to the hanger and fuel area. Something started crisscrossing the runway ahead. At first I thought it was a deer, but instead it was a big dog being chased around by a man. Some dogs chase cars; this one liked airplanes. I waited until the man had it under control before taxiing to the fuel pit. I was glad it didn't take too long. (I didn't want to embarrass myself by running out of fuel on the runway.)

Jerry Adkinson, one of the nicest people I met on this entire trip, was standing next to the gas pump waiting for me when I shut down the engine. He pumped forty-one gallons of fuel into the forty-six-gallon tank. I was glad I had decided not to fly around the field before landing.

Obviously, Jerry likes old airplanes. With a big smile, he said, "I can't hardly believe it, this is the second old round engine airplane that's stopped here today." From his description I think the other one was a gull wing Stinson.

After fueling we talked about the beauty of older airplanes, older motorcycles, and mature women (pilot stuff). From the questions he asked it was obvious that he was genuinely interested in the Stearman and seemed envious of my trip.

He asked, "Have you ever flown to Galesburg up north for their annual Fly-In?"

"Yeah, I sure have. Stopped by there on my way to Denver ten years ago when I first bought this Stearman," I replied. "It was late on a Saturday evening when we got there, since we had spent most of Friday repairing a leaking oil cooler."

"There must be a hundred Stearmans that show up there every year."

"It just so happens that we were Stearman number 108 to register for the show in 1990. There were still about seventy-five biplanes on the ground when we landed and it was the first time I'd ever seen that many multi-colored Stearmans at one time. It sure was a beautiful sight."

The annual Stearman Fly-In at Galesburg attracts the best Stearmans in the world, and it's a pilgrimage that every devout Stearman owner will make sometime in his life, if possible.

Jerry asked first, and then captured a few pictures of Le Beast and myself, then all three of us. He promised to send me some copies after he had them developed; I had hoped that he would. I told him I would plan to stop here on the way back and give him a ride when it wasn't so windy and we both had more time.

# CHAPTER 25

**WHEN I WENT** inside to pay for the fuel, I was pleasantly surprised to find that here, in the middle of what seemed nowhere at first, was a restoration facility for the Beechcraft T-34 Mentor. I had been an instructor pilot for our Aero Club T-34 while serving in the U.S. Air Force. It brought back a lot of pleasant flying memories as well as mixed emotions about that Vietnam era. The pleasant memories were of the carefree days that we would fly the T-34s low over the Black Hills of South Dakota, taking pictures of the donkey herds in the valleys. The mixed and painful emotions were associated with the thousands of Americans who came back from Southeast Asia in caskets.

The first prototypes of the T-34 were flown in 1948 and they were designed to replace the North American AT-6, but it was not used as a trainer by the Air Force until 1953. The Navy and the Air Force found the T34 Mentor to be an exceptional inter-service trainer aircraft. The Navy received its first 423 planes in 1954.

Both services found the T-34 was a rugged and very reliable plane, and it was used as a primary and intermediate trainer before pilots phased into jet aircraft. For twenty-five years, thousands of Air Force and Navy pilots earned their wings flying in the T-34. Most pilots who have flown them agree that they handle like a dream in the air and are very forgiving on takeoff and landing. But they were somewhat limited and underpowered, with only a 225 hp Continental engine.

By the mid-1970s, the Air Force went to the T-37 all-jet fleet, while the Navy went to the T-34C model with a Pratt and Whitney PT6A turboprop engine which had about twice the power of the piston engine. The Navy and some Latin American countries are still using this model as a trainer and as a light attack aircraft. I sure wouldn't pass up a chance to fly a C model if the opportunity ever presented itself.

It's a great airplane and I have a firsthand appreciation for this fine aircraft. As a Stearman restorer, I can appreciate the workmanship being performed at Tuscola airport and I was very pleased to see these old airplanes being rebuilt and coming to life again. Like the Stearman, it has become quite valuable as a superb acrobatic and sport plane.

I enjoyed my visit at Tuscola and could have happily lingered longer, but the time came to clear prop again. The '66 VW bus I saw on landing—with the peace symbol painted on the side—told me I was back on my time schedule, so I didn't wind the clock.

After departing Tuscola around noon, my initial plan was to fly somewhat south of route 36 again and work my way around the Springfield, Illinois airspace. It was still hot and windy and I was starting to get that windburn, sunburned, raccoon-eyed, barnstormer suntan. I was looking too good to pass up. We were just about halfway to St. Francis at that point. No turning back now; I was starting to get my second wind. And, with a full tank of petrol, I was looking forward to the rest of the trip.

Relaxing and leveling off at one thousand feet or so, the air seemed a little smoother. From somewhere afar, the aroma of lilac combined with a sweet smell of burning oil from the engine, and awakened my senses with sheer intoxication. The gentle breeze whirling throughout the cockpit flooded my memory with visions of a beautiful young lady swaying past on a late summer's eve. Closing my eyes, I reached out my hand through the soft white bed of passing clouds to absorb the lush green farmland below, gently swaying in the wind on this peaceful summer day, and was at peace with Mother Nature once again.

Passing by Springfield and Jacksonville, we soon crossed the Illinois River. Shortly thereafter, with Pittsville a few miles in the background, I could see the flatland area of the Mississippi. I knew that Mark Twain's Hannibal, Missouri, would soon appear on the horizon. I was hot and thirsty and ready for another pit stop, so I planned an early refueling at the Hannibal airport.

# CHAPTER 26

**THE GOOD FOLKS** at Hannibal Airport have an excellent reputation for helping biplane pilots and providing shelter for their planes. Word travels fast in the Stearman world concerning which airports are the best for weary travelers. Le Beast had spent a stormy November night here on its way to Maryland a few years earlier. Some of the larger airports tend to cater more to the charter type of aircraft than to small planes. This is not so at Hannibal. Hannibal is a small aircraft, people-oriented airport.

No sooner had I landed and shut everything down than I noticed another dog. A beautiful Siberian Husky with sparkling blue eyes sat at the corner of my left elevator wagging her tail. She seemed to be saying, "Welcome to Hannibal." I immediately nicknamed her Hannibal Hanna. After climbing down off the wing and giving her a pat on the head, she slowly sauntered back towards the terminal as if inviting me over for a cup of tea. I followed her over to the terminal and received instructions from her humans on how to fuel.

It was close to noon and I thought about taking an hour or so for a relaxing lunch break in town. But I was running a little late and knew I had one more refuel stop somewhere in Missouri before I could make it all the way to Concordia. I ate an energy bar from my flight bag instead, washed it down with a Dr. Pepper, then refueled and decided to take a longer break at my next stop. Maybe the next airport would have an air-conditioned res-taurant and a sassy waitress to serve iced tea and a club sandwich—every pilot's dream.

I thought about calling Jackie in Kansas City to get a local weather report, but I couldn't think of an acceptable way of starting a conversation. I might have been opening a Pandora's box of emotions that I didn't want to drag along on the trip. The guilt of not calling and asking her to meet me in St. Francis was already beginning to weigh on me. So I mumbled under my breath, "Maybe later."

After a quick check with Flight Services on the weather and the unrelenting wind gods, I departed, knowing I would stop here again on my return trip. I wanted to visit a little longer with Ms. Hannibal Hanna and these good folks. And, time permitting, visit the Mark Twain museum again.

So clear prop, we're outta here. No need to wind the clock; saw a 1959 Chevrolet convertible driving around the airport earlier.

# CHAPTER 27

**SOMEWHERE ACROSS MISSOURI,** the farmland began to change into a large checkerboard landscape. Most of the fields were perfect little squares with an old farmhouse and red-roofed barns in the middle. The settlers had originally established their homesteads in one-mile square patterns, using basically a north-south design. We were getting closer to Kansas.

Passing Chillicothe, Missouri, memories of stopping here with Jim Walters on our way back to Denver in 1990 came freshly to mind. We had just attended the Annual Stearman Fly-In at Galesburg, Illinois, and were following John Grace on his way back to St. Francis in his Stearman. We had to wake up an older gentleman sleeping in a trailer to get fuel. I had lost a pair of goggles here while doing a carrier-type takeoff with my head too far above the windshield.

Checking the fuel gauge just north of Kansas City, I decided to stop at Cameron, Missouri, for food and gas. It was a nice airport and the manager, Steve Fox, was there to greet me as soon as I landed and taxied up to the fuel pumps.

The first thing he said after I shut down the engine was, "Man, she's a beauty. What year is it?"

"It's a 1942/2000," I replied. Then I clarified, "It was built in 1942, but completely restored by 2000."

"Looks brand new. You want to top her off with fuel?"

"Sure, and I'll need two quarts of Aero Shell oil if you have it."

"Will you need a cab to go into town for lunch? All we have in the office is a snack machine."

"Thanks, but I'm on a tight schedule to get to Kansas before dark."

He and his wife had just started a flight school here and had great hopes for the future of general aviation. They had one of the largest German Shepherd dogs I've ever seen. This half horse/half wolf with barn door ears was friendly enough, but he liked to herd me around like a Border Collie herds sheep. He was obviously enjoying this little intimidation game. Over the years I've owned two very large Great Danes, but I still gave this dog all the space he needed. By the time I left we were friends…I think.

Steve offered to put the plane inside for the night. I thanked him, but told him I had already made plans to stop overnight in Concordia. I told him I might take him up on the offer on the return trip. He showed me how to use the refueling system in case he wasn't there. In my haste I hadn't observed any significant time changes.

# CHAPTER 28

**IT WAS LATE** afternoon when I crossed the Missouri River into Kansas and the sun was getting lower on the horizon, causing a slight glare. Flying around the St Joseph control area, I turned on the hand-held radio and dialed in the approach frequency, to stay clear of other aircraft coming in from the West.

Moving my finger along the chart, I realized that we would soon be over Hiawatha. My mom was born about twenty miles south in Horton, Kansas. It felt like I was coming back home again. Just outside Hiawatha, flying over the graveyard, I waved to those relatives who have passed; lots of Cherokee ancestors are buried in Brown County.

Now that I was back in Kansas and flying along Route 36, I knew Le Beast could almost find its own way back to St. Francis. But I kept my finger on the chart anyway. It had long since become habit again. It was still hot and the wind wasn't giving me a break, so I needed to keep tabs on fuel consumption.

For a brief moment I gave serious consideration to flying on to Smith Center or Norton, but I knew I could find shelter for the plane in Concordia. Stearman pilots and their planes can always find room and board here. For many years it has been a welcome stopover point for Stearman pilots en route to the Annual Fly-In at Galesburg.

After passing Marysville, I decided to follow the power lines and then the railroad tracks to Concordia. This path would take me past the Washington County airport, then to Palmer, Clifton, Clyde, and straight to Concordia.

With a bright orange-red sun blazing directly on the horizon, following the power lines was a little tricky at first. After passing the Washington Airport, I began following the railroad tracks instead. The tracks soon turned into an old railroad bed without rails and they became even harder to follow than the power lines. The tracks soon disappeared completely, and I scolded myself, "Here you go again, Russ, pushing limits. Didn't you learn anything after almost running out of gas in Illinois? Do you want to add 'getting lost' to your little bag of tricks today?"

I thought about the first Heartland barnstormers as I flew the last few miles just above the trees, searching for the same landmarks; I felt sure they had encountered similar obstacles daily. While gradually working my way from small town to small town, the sun was constantly in my eyes, but it was hard to whine too much. Just being there and being able to fly into a large fading sunset somehow overshadowed the minor inconvenience of it all.

Finally, I saw the water tower at the airport; what a welcome sight. Circling to land, with fuel to spare, I smiled and thought to myself, *God, it feels good to be back in Kansas.*

# CHAPTER 29

**THE AIRPORT STAFF** was still there and willing to help. They had built another hanger in recent years and there was plenty of room for the night. They were getting ready to leave for the day, so I decided to wait until morning to refuel. St. Francis was about two hours west, and there would be plenty of time before leaving tomorrow morning.

I thought again about calling Jackie, while pushing the Stearman into the hanger. I was remembering when she had flown up here from Kansas City and stayed overnight. Those were good times for the both of us. Then I thought, *If I call she'd probably just hang up after she finds out I'm in Concordia and on my way to St. Francis without her.* I didn't want to take the chance of ruining any hopes we'd settle our differences later, so I decided to wait. Instead, I hoped that she would show up in St. Francis on her own sometime over the weekend.

After cleaning the oil and dust off the plane with a spray wax, I caught a ride into town with a local teacher who was working part-time at the airport in exchange for flying time. The restaurant at the motel had closed for the day. In typical Kansas fashion, he insisted on taking me back in town to get a burger and a milkshake.

We talked about flying and, of course, the upcoming St. Francis Fly-In. I promised him a Stearman ride for his hospitality as he dropped me off at the motel.

I retrieved my flight bag from his back seat, checked in, and collapsed on the bed for a few minutes. Before showering off the daily dust, grit, sweat, and oil, I unpacked my flight bag for the day. At that point I almost panicked when I realized that I was missing my treasured A-2 flight jacket. Tracing back in my mind I realized it was probably in the back seat of a teacher's car somewhere in Kansas.

As it turned out, the motel manager knew the teacher. After several calls, we made contact and determined that, yes, it was in his back seat and, yes, he would be happy to drive twenty-five miles back to town to drop it off. I offered to pay him for his trouble, but once again he declined. Then I promised him *two* Stearman rides if he came to St. Francis over the weekend. I think he knew how much I valued the flight jacket.

I called home and discovered that Mel had gone to her girlfriend's house for the evening. She had tried unsuccessfully to talk her mother into buying her an airline ticket to St. Francis via Denver for the Fly-In. Guess she had advanced through her anger and bargaining stages and needed a sympathetic ear to lean on for the night. I knew how desperately she wanted to be with me and it bothered me a lot, but I hoped she would eventually understand and not hold any harsh feelings towards me later. I really understood her disappointment and felt bad for her.

After showering and putting lotion on my raccoon tan lines, I was more than ready to hit the sack. I was tired but happy, and looking forward to sleeping in, having a late breakfast, and flying on to St. Francis tomorrow. Overall, it had been another good day and I had made some new friends along the way, but I longed to hug my girls.

# CHAPTER 30

## *FRIDAY—DAY THREE*

**FRIDAY MORNING I** woke up to a familiar rattle somewhere in the room. In my groggy state of mind I first thought, *Rattlesnake*, but then realized it was the window rattling instead. Talk about waking up in a hurry!

Knowing it was the "Winds of Kansas," I looked out the window to see the trees whipping back and forth in the motel parking lot. The wind gods were coming back in full glory. It was time to hit the road again. But first I needed lots of coffee and some Kansas steak and eggs.

I remembered having another late breakfast here a few years back with John Grace and his wife Elsie. We had all stopped here overnight on our way back from Galesburg. They were really enjoying the trip and John was excited about a new GPS he had in his Stearman.

Then I thought to myself, *John, why the hell did you bring me back to Kansas? Maybe I'm going to witness some tragic event; or maybe stop something awful from happening; or maybe it's because I'm supposed to do something of great significance; or maybe...this is my last flight? Maybe, maybe, maybe!*

I wasn't really worried or concerned for my well-being, just curious. It's not my nature to dwell on negative thoughts too long, so I didn't. Whatever happened later, happened.

After breakfast I checked out and asked at the front desk about a cab. The manager had some business in town and volunteered to drop me by the airport. Talk about customer service! She said she also wanted to see the biplane that I had talked (and talked) about while checking in yesterday.

The people in Concordia like old biplanes. They even have an old 1930s Lincoln Page biplane in the downtown museum. Whether driving or flying, I usually try to stop by and see this rare bird if I'm in the area and have a few minutes to spare.

By the time I arrived at the airport I already knew the wind was stronger today than it had been the past two days. I sure was glad the plane had been inside overnight.

When we pushed it outside the hanger for fueling it immediately weather-vanned into the already strong south wind. We had to place chocks behind the front wheels and tail wheel to keep it from moving backwards. Knowing this was a little more than just a normal Kansas wind, I decided to put it back in the hanger and refuel inside when I was ready to leave.

Another pilot at the airport was already checking on the weather and winds for the day when I went into the terminal office. When he found out that I was headed west he said, "You're in for a wild ride, cowboy." The gusty winds along the route were scheduled to stay above twenty to twenty-five knots from the south-southwest for the rest of the morning and then get stronger in the afternoon.

Knowing that it was almost two hundred miles from Concordia to St. Francis, I decided to refuel somewhere along the way, just in case. No need to tempt fate a second day. I asked the airport staff which airports along the route had north-south runways and fuel for sure. They agreed on Norton airport, but suggested that I call first to see if anyone was there today. Since the airport manager is also the local spray pilot, he might not be around on such a windy day.

I called ahead and they promised to have someone stay around for another hour or so. Especially since I was flying a Stearman to St. Francis. They also suggested it was a "little windy" for a biplane there today. I assured them I would be there or call back if I decided to turn around instead.

Around nine a.m. Le Beast and I reluctantly exited the hanger for the second time. I stayed in the cockpit while two other men pulled us outside by the wing tips and pointed us into that gusty Kansas wind. They held on while I yelled "Clear prop!", then pushed the starter button to wake up 450 sleepy horses.

Before takeoff I noticed a 1953 Cessna 180A that had just landed, and the ground crew was rushing out to hold the wings down while the pilot slowly taxied in. It reminded me of the Cessna 180 I sold to buy this Stearman, and it looked like it had just rolled off the show room floor. I thought to myself, *this must be the year 1953; time to wind the clock again, exactly eight times for the day.* Then, since I had only two hundred miles to fly and about twenty more years to go back in time, I decided to wind it only six times and see what happened.

# CHAPTER 31

**LEAVING CONCORDIA AT** mid-field, I spurred Le Beast into the air and we made probably the shortest takeoff of the trip. It usually takes around seven hundred feet to get airborne at that altitude, but we were in the air and climbing in less than five hundred feet. As soon as I was airborne I knew the wind was indeed more southwest than south, and, with that much headwind, it had been a good decision to stop for fuel at Norton.

Placing my finger back on the chart I decided to follow the same railroad track and then a power line to Smith Center. I soon ran out of railroad tracks to follow; then started following the power lines that were all but invisible in the early morning light. However, I could occasionally see the towers between the lines glistening like crosses in the sun; they were leading me west across the prairie landscape. I smiled knowing this was what flying had been like to the first barnstormers.

Checking my ground speed as I passed Smith Center, I realized the wind was getting stronger. I hoped the airport runway at Norton was wide enough to forgive the tricky landing we were about to make.

Crossing over the center of the airport at Norton I saw that the windsock was standing straight out. I knew the wind was at least twenty-five knots and it was gusting out of the southwest about forty-five degrees from the right side of the narrow active runway.

I set up for a straight in, powered, tail-low, wheel landing with the right wing cocked down enough to stay straight with the runway. After passing the landing threshold I started easing off the power at 1500 rpm...1300 rpm ...1100...900... then lowered the right landing gear slowly to the ground. Slowly but surely, the wheel finally contacted the runway and I held it on one gear until we slowed down enough to let it settle on both wheels.

I offset the tendency for the plane to shift to the right and into the wind by adding more right aileron and a little left brake. Then, when I slowed down enough that it was somewhat under control, I eased the power all the way back and pulled the tail wheel firmly on the ground and started adding a little more left brake to keep it straight. At first it handled somewhat like a confused squirrel, but it gradually slowed down; then we were safely on the ground again.

Slightly tail-low, wheel landings have always worked best for me in most crosswind situations.

Each Stearman pilot has his own opinion and technique for landings. I respect them all. I just know what works best for me. Looking towards the hanger and seeing several people watching me and shaking their heads, I wondered how much money had changed hands at our expense.

With the best grin I could muster, I climbed down from the walkway on the left wing and stood on shaky legs. "Thanks" seemed like such an inadequate expression of appreciation for their waiting and providing the gas that we so desperately needed to get to St. Francis. But, they accepted my gratitude and showed me around their hanger and repair shop where they were rebuilding another tail wheel plane. General aviation will never die as long as good American warriors like these keep fighting the battle of survival. After tying the plane down and taking a short break, they passed the fuel hose up to the front cockpit for refueling the wing tank. Then it was time to grit the teeth and fish tail out behind another windy Kansas pilot for more fun and games.

The most significant indicator of time I had observed, while on the ground, was Le Beast. For a few minutes it was the center of attention at Norton airport, so 1942 it is. "Clear Prop. St. Francis, here we come."

# CHAPTER 32

**ANOTHER PILOT GETTING** ready for takeoff was flying a relatively new single engine Cessna 210. I remember saying aloud, "It certainly would be a shame to see that beauty rolled into a ball across the airport." After a long, fast takeoff roll, the plane suddenly lifted into the air, then shifted to a forty five-degree angle as soon as he cleared the runway. He immediately pulled up the retractable gear and wobbled his way towards the South. I knew that we would receive this same type of treatment from Mother Nature during our takeoff.

Keeping the tail wheel low in the beginning roll down the runway, Le Beast was soon firmly on the main gear and ready for another one-wheel take-off using lots of right aileron and rudder. As soon as the plane lifted from the runway the wind did the same number on us that it did on the Cessna. The first one hundred feet slammed me up and down and around in the cockpit like a limp doll. Then, after shifting into the headwind with a strong right rudder, the plane suddenly lifted almost straight up like a fast moving freight elevator. I gradually leveled off at five hundred feet under full power and thought aloud, "Oooh man, this is supposed to be fun."

The guys at Concordia and Norton were right; it was a wild cowboy ride and a little windy for flying a biplane that day.

While following Highway 36 west again and noticing the wind howling across the wheat fields, thoughts of "amber waves of grain" became more surreal than comforting. It was more like a "mad sea of grain."

Mother Nature seemed a little pissed that day. Looking towards the southwest I noticed a wide area of dust blowing up from the Goodland, Kansas, direction. It had to be ten to twenty miles wide and five hundred feet high. It looked like a picture from the depression era.

While bouncing past Bird City, I tuned in the Cheyenne County Airport frequency on the handheld radio. This would be my first radio contact with the ground since leaving Maryland on Wednesday. I had thoroughly enjoyed being able to fly fifteen hundred miles with my finger on the chart and not having the FAA in my ears for a change. It reminded me of some of my first cross-country flying in a J-3 Cub. It was a great basic VFR navigation refresher!

The airport reported that the winds at the airport were blowing out of the southwest twenty-five to twenty-nine knots, and gusting to thirty-four knots. A good, hot, dusty wind is the sign of early summer, but I wasn't overly concerned about landing at St. Francis. With three wide grass runways forming a triangle at the airport, I knew I could find a safe place to land almost directly into the southwest wind.

After drifting across the power lines and floating gently onto the southwest grass runway, I realized this would be one of the shortest three-point landings I've ever made in Kansas. Under no-wind conditions it would have taken about eight hundred feet or so to land a Stearman at St. Francis on this hot day. But today it took only a few hundred feet to slowly plant Le Beast on the sod then brake to a stop after an almost perfect three-point landing. Just before contact with the runway, I could almost feel the soft prairie grass quietly swishing past all three wheels at the same time. Too bad nobody but a prairie dog was there to witness this absolutely splendiferous feat.

While taxiing towards tie-down at 12:35 p.m., I calculated that I had just flown the Stearman fifteen hundred miles in seventeen hours over a period of three days. We had averaged 88 mph and were thirty-five minutes late on my estimated time of arrival. But I thought that just might be acceptable, by barnstorming standards. Especially with having to fight a wind in my face the whole trip.

I really hadn't anticipated the wind staying on the nose of the plane all the way there. It didn't let up once. The only time it changed was when it increased. I had flown, for the most part, in the middle of a large, windy, high-pressure system. The weather at times was unbearably hot and dry, but overall it was good barnstorming weather.

Nonetheless, it still felt great being in St. Francis.

# PART III

## - THE STEARMAN FLY-IN -

# CHAPTER 33

**THE FIRST PERSON** I saw on the ground was John Grace's oldest son Robert, arriving in his golf cart. He had a big smile on his face; he always has a nice smile to greet everyone. Robert is one of the most gregarious and multi-talented fliers I've ever met. He is an exceptional Stearman flier, dedicated balloonist, expert skydiver, and a highly experienced spray pilot. If it can be flown, sailed, lifted, or driven through the air, Robert can do it with confidence and ease. He is well liked throughout the aviation community and highly respected by his fellow fliers. He is truly a seat-of-the-pants renaissance pilot.

We shook hands and he said, "It's good to see you back in St. Francis, Russ. We missed seeing you the past couple of summers."

My reply was, "Not half as much as I've missed being here."

It always feels like a family reunion when I come to St. Francis. The entire Grace family, the balloon pilots, the skydivers, the good citizens of St. Francis, and my fellow Stearman pilots—one and all—treat each other like long-lost relatives.

He nodded and smiled, but I thought that he probably didn't fully understand how much I had missed St. Francis. And, until I got there, I didn't realize just how much I had missed it, either. The clear blue Kansas sky and the wheat-covered landscape was a welcome sight.

"Well, it looks like you're the first one here," he commented.

"I would have been here yesterday if Mother Nature and the Kansas wind had cooperated a little better."

"The wind's not too bad today. You should have been here earlier in the week. It was blowing constantly at thirty to forty knots for about two days."

"I know. I flew in that wind for the past three days. But, as you know, I'd fly in any kind of weather just to get here before Eric,"—our good friend and a competitive barnstormer.

We both laughed.

We talked about the family aerial spraying business, and he said it had been a very dry year, but the south winds had unexpectedly brought in wheat aphids so he was still in business. During all this I wanted to tell him the chief reason I came back to St. Francis. I wanted to tell him about the dream, but I wasn't sure if I should or not. I decided to wait and let the weekend take its course.

After unloading my baggage I went into the terminal and found John Grace's younger son Richard at the weather station shaking his head. He said the winds and temperature had been a little high that spring. Presently the wind was twenty-eight to thirty-two knots, gusting to about thirty-six, and the temperature was ninety-four degrees.

He said, "Welcome back to Kansas, Russ, where it's a little hot, a bit dry, and a tad windy."

I've always enjoyed his dry sense of humor and Mark Twain wit, mixed with gracious mannerism. He has an instinctive and untiring way of placing people at ease while making them feel welcome at the annual Fly-In year after year.

At first, I had noticed only one other Stearman at the airport when I arrived. It was the blue and yellow 225 Stearman owned by Dr. Curt Kimball (we call him Doc) from Sterling, Colorado. Then, while walking past the hangers, I noticed the other yellow 220 Stearman, belonging to Grace Flying Service. It was the last remaining spray plane that John Grace had retired years earlier. It is now just a sport plane again, and everyone enjoys seeing it still flying.

It was very fitting that these two planes were the first ones here today. A few years earlier, Doc Kimball had landed here while working his way around thunderstorms going back to Sterling from the Bartlesville, Oklahoma, biplane Fly-In. Seeing the three wide, sod-grass runways and another Stearman, he knew he had a new mission in life.

After talking to John Grace they decided that the First Annual St. Francis Stearman Fly-In would be held the following year. They knew there would be at least those two Stearmans there.

# CHAPTER 34

**THE EMPIRE MOTEL** and Dusty Farmer Restaurant are within walking distance of the airport. I had called ahead and reserved a two-bedroom unit just in case Jackie showed up over the weekend. Even though I was apprehensive about seeing her, I hoped she would come. It just wouldn't be the same without her. I decided to stretch my legs and go check in and take a short lunch break. And then it would be time for a siesta under the wings while waiting for the rest of the Stearman pilots to arrive.

On the way over to the motel I noticed a bright red Ford Roadster convertible parked at the service station across the street. When I inquired inside about the owner of the car, the clerk said an older gentleman with a gray beard wearing a baseball cap had been driving it. But nobody seemed to know where he was at that time. Maybe he was walking around the town or the airport. It was a beauty; it had 1928 Kansas license plates and it seemed so factory fresh I could almost smell the new upholstery. I had planned to arrive in St. Francis in the 1930s, but 1928 was just fine. Glad I had wound the clock only six times that morning.

After checking in with Darrel Johnson, the manager at the motel, I walked back to the terminal to take a trip down memory lane by looking over the picture albums displayed of previous Fly-Ins. I enjoyed seeing the pictures of the Stearmans I had flown here in the past. The first one, with a 220 hp engine; the second one, with 300 hp; and the 450 hp (Le Beast) I now have. There's no such thing as too much horsepower to a Stearman pilot. It's always exciting to re-visit and observe the history being captured in these albums.

By three p.m. the wind was down to about 20 mph, and a few other planes started drifting in, but still no other Stearmans. I had talked with Eric a few days earlier and he should have been here by now. Hoped everything was okay with him and his biplane. He also flies a big red Stearman, trimmed with a black stripe down the side of the fuselage.

Sometimes dressed in the same type of knee-high leather flying boots worn by his grandfather, he takes a lot of good-natured ribbing from his fellow barnstormers. One year at the Loveland, Colorado, air show Jim Walters asked him, "Hey Eric, can I borrow your boots for next weekend? I need them to break in my polo pony."

I smiled knowing I had once again arrived ahead of him.

# CHAPTER 35

**ST. FRANCIS ISN'T** just another typical mid-western town. Geographically it is, but there's something very special about this town that keeps everyone coming back here every second weekend in June. That something is the warm, sincere hospitality that the people extend to everyone who attends the Fly-In. I've never met a person in this town who wasn't friendly and helpful to a fault. Every business and every person in town seems willing to go out of their way to extend support during the entire weekend. We have always been treated like personal guests, and spending time there is always more like attending a family reunion.

Having lived half my life in the West, there will always be a special place in my heart and soul for the Heartland. Year after year, what really pulls me back is the open beauty of the land and looking down and seeing the canvas of so many colors. For miles and miles, as far as I can see, the horizon is multi-colored in gold and green with soft shades of brown mingled in. Even high above, I sometimes can smell the perfume of wildflowers or the muskiness of freshly cut hay. I always enjoy the freedom of flying here, but what I treasure most is the warmth and friendliness of the people. I take a lot of pride in knowing that I have roots here in Kansas and hope that someday I'll be able to spend more time here.

The Stearman Fly-In at St. Francis brings an assorted group of people to town each year. It attracts Stearman enthusiasts, other airplane pilots, balloonists, skydivers, visitors, and local folks. And most of these people have experienced, or will experience, the thrill of a biplane ride.

This Fly-In is one of the best-kept secrets in the Stearman world. It is not an air show, just a small Fly-In. One year we had twelve Stearmans show up and another year we had only four. Everyone hopes it will remain this small so we can continue to enjoy it without having to restrict any of the future activities.

There's really no official beginning or end to the Fly-In. It's just a weekend in June that has been set-aside by these good folks for all those who want to come and enjoy flying, ballooning, and skydiving.

For the area Stearman pilots, coming to this place is almost like a pilgrimage. Their being there in St. Francis is like dying and going to biplane heaven. This large grass runway setup cannot to be found anywhere else in the area. There's seldom a time that they can't take off or land safely into the strongest of the winds. This is a big plus for those who believe in the ground looping reputation that sometimes haunts the Stearman.

Around four p.m. I saw two biplanes on the horizon coming from the west. I knew one of the planes would be Eric's 300 Stearman. He was already testing the smoker with an occasional puff in preparation for his fly-by. As they flew past the terminal, I saw it was indeed Eric's plane, with an older Eaglerock in tow.

After landing he waved and flashed a big grin as he taxied by. I was glad to see him also. We both knew we'd have fun competing against each other over the weekend.

Over the years Eric and I have had a lot of fun barnstorming together throughout the Heartland. One year we did a WWI dogfight routine at the Sterling, Colorado, air show. We mesmerized and scared the hell out of a lot of people that day. It was completely unrehearsed, but probably one of our better routines. We were invincible, much like we still are today. Signing autographs after the show was a gigantic ego booster.

# CHAPTER 36

**HAVING STEARMANS, BALLOONS,** and skydivers in the air together at St. Francis might sound a little tricky or even dangerous. But we've never had any serious problems with all of this activity going on at the same time. We've been very fortunate that everyone just tries to relax and have a good time while showing due respect to fellow fliers.

Robert Grace deserves a lot of credit for coordinating most of the activity that takes place at the airport. His experience as a pilot, balloonist, and skydiver gives him a good overall perspective and he is always a spokesperson for safety first.

Another activity that helps pull all the fliers together is the welcoming party held at Robert and his wife Debbie's house on Friday evening. Once again, the beautiful weather for this night seems willing to cooperate.

Since a lot of us have flown in and have no transportation without wings, we walk through the streets of this quaint town to a beautifully restored Victorian home where we gather together. And what a party it is! The noise from the party comes to my ears a few blocks away and I can hear the hum of conversation with the occasional outburst of laughter.

The next sense to awaken is smell. This is one of the finest catered affairs I've ever attended, and the food is abundant. Fancy little appetizers, tempting side dishes, and various smoked meats for sandwiches. Not to mention some of the homemade treats the local townsfolk have so generously thrown in.

Turning the corner onto their street, I see all of the people gathered into various groups. The skydivers in one group tell jokes raunchy enough to make even another skydiver blush, and  stories of near death and peril that become more elaborate with each turn. The pilots nearby try to outdo the skydivers in tall tales but get nowhere near to matching them in vulgarity. The balloon pilots are in their own group with equally outrageous stories.

As the evening wears on, the groups will merge and everyone will be walking around like one large family. Robert and Debbie are very congenial hosts and make it appear effortless to provide such a relaxed and warm atmosphere. They even have a place for the kids to play in the back yard. Probably to keep them occupied until the death, peril, and jokes have worn down.

Before the party, a group of skydivers always descend on an open field across the street from the Grace's house. Sometimes there might be eight or ten parachutes in the air at one time lining up to land in that small area. These guys are good! The multi-colored chutes being highlighted by the fading Kansas sunset was a beautiful sight to see as they slowly drifted down.

One year the jump plane was down for maintenance and we dropped four skydivers from our Stearman. That was the first time I let anyone jump from my plane, but it wouldn't be the last. From time to time I've asked several skydivers, including Jackie, what it's like to skydive. Most of them have the same response: "It's a real hoot, man. It's bitchin', man. It's a real rush, man. It's cool!" Sounds like fun to me.

A few years ago I asked Jackie if she could define for me, in terms I would understand, what it's like to skydive for the first time. She said she would have to think about it. She knew I wouldn't accept just a short reply, so later she wrote:

**Dear Dad,**
*Year after year I had driven or flown to see you and the wonderful pilots of the infamous St. Francis Fly-In. Year after year I saw Robert Grace and the other skydivers with their flashy jumpsuits and even more brilliant canopies looking death in the face and laughing (so I thought). I tried so hard to convince myself this was absolute insanity. Being a pilot myself, how could I ever justify jumping out of the proverbial perfectly good airplane? Well, with*

absolutely no forethought that that year was going to be the year, I suffered a mental lapse and decided to just go for it.

Before I knew what was happening, I was paying my money and being told to come back and suit up in two hours. I felt like a lunatic. I thought to myself, "What in the heck are you doing? Why now? Why are you such a damned adrenaline junkie? You are just like your dad!" As the time got closer and closer, I felt sicker and sicker. I have never had my heart beat so hard and so fast and with such terror. Yet I knew with absolute certainty that this was something that I had to do.

As in a dream, I ventured toward the open hanger where the skydivers held camp and met my tandem instructor right on time and was given the basics about how I would be attached to him. He told me what I was to expect once we got in the airplane. He showed me how to just relax and fall once we hit the air and how I was supposed to help him to steer the canopy once it opened. Signing the waivers and listening to him talk was all so unreal and happened so fast. Before I knew it, we were loading into the plane and waving a final goodbye to everyone. If I remember correctly, you weren't there because you were getting ready for the balloon burst. It was probably *best, because you probably had more fear in your eyes than I had in mine.*

*The higher and higher the plane went and the closer to twelve thousand feet above the ground we became, the more and more certain I was of my impending death. Cold terror had completely taken over. I was driven at this point by something so deep inside that I can't easily relate to it today.*

*"Are you ready to skydive?" my tandem partner yelled at me above the noise of the Cessna 182. "Okay," was all I could manage to say. He strapped me to his front so that I was facing away and in the same direction as he. He pulled and tugged and buckled and adjusted until I was tightly secured right next to his front. We moved as one toward the opening of the plane and the pilot yelled, "Door!" This was the indication that it was okay for my snuggly fit counterpart to open the airplane door, peer over my shoulder and look down to find the spot where they would still be digging for my shattered bone fragments a month later. He happily found it right away, yelled at the pilot to cut the engine back and indicated for me to step one of my feet outside of the plane onto the strut of the wing.*

*Dad, I cannot tell you how terrified I was. How sad and scared and alone. Maybe if I had not* been feeling all of that, the next feeling that came to me would not have been so intense. I put my foot out on the strut and became so scared that I backed up hard into him. He was going to have none of that and, being used to idiots such as myself, he pushed himself hard into me, throwing us both tumbling briefly out of the door.

Nothing, and I mean absolutely nothing, has ever compared to the intensity of what I felt all within about five seconds. Every fear, every heartache, every insecurity that I have ever had in my young years was gone in an instant. I was untouchable. I was invincible. I was free. It was surreal. The earth moving toward me (because I was suspended and everything else was moving). The wind blowing so fiercely into my ears that I could hear nothing. The knowledge that I was completely free from any attachments, real or imagined. No responsibility. No care. Just to fly above the earth. I realized that these daring skydivers did not face dying when they did this incredible thing. They faced living. And then it was over. Almost.

At about four thousand feet above the ground, my tandem master, who I had long forgotten about, deployed the parachute. I think that it was about a week before my thighs recovered from the harness! The canopy was breathtaking. The view was breathtaking. The slow flight *down to earth with no motor, no enclosure. Just a huge inflated fabric wing above our heads. It was very beautiful. The canopy ride down was definitely an experience in itself. But the feeling of the free-fall is something unforgettable. Consuming and addictive are those forty-five seconds where you are absolutely more in control of your destiny than at almost any other time in your life. Amazing!*

*I wish that I could get in your brain and help you to understand. Maybe someday you will if you don't already. The only other thing that I have to share with you is about the day that I jumped from Eric's Stearman while you were flying right beside. I have no spiritual description of it other than it was just a plain kick to know that you were there in the sky with me and I could probably still instill fear into the heart of my father. I hope you could see me smiling as I let go and looked back at where you were!*

*I love you and I hope this helps you understand.*

*Your daughter in skin and soul,*

*Jackie.*

During the party I finally had an opportunity to talk to Robert about his dad and the dream. I told him the entire story of how his dad had influenced my coming back to St. Francis. I think I caught him by surprise because he was silent at first. And then so was I.

After a moment, I suggested that maybe my father's recent death and my wanting to come back so desperately might have triggered such a dream. We both just nodded and, then we changed the subject. Maybe we were both still missing our dads too much to discuss it. I just thought he might like to know the whole story.

Just before dark I noticed the wind had calmed considerably and that two late-arriving Stearmans were in the landing pattern. Several pilots decided it was the right time to leave the party and go back to the airport. We usually check on the planes before calling it a day.

It's not unusual to see Stearmans flying at this late hour if they have adequate instruments and lighting. One year, at twilight, two pilots flew their Stearmans just above the trees over the golf course while the rest of the fliers were enjoying dinner inside the clubhouse. Everyone seemed to enjoy their little cat and mouse flying routine, but what they really enjoyed was seeing the bluish yellow flames from the exhaust pipes as they headed back to the airport. (Actually, these two pilots were just following protocol. The previous year a group of skydivers had landed on the eighteenth green, for all the fliers' entertainment.)

While walking back to the motel from the airport with several pilots, we discussed how good it was to be there and how much fun we were having. We agreed that this was definitely the highlight of the year and ranked right up there with great sex. One of the female pilots said it was better, and everyone laughed, except her male companion. He walked several steps behind us the rest of the way to the motel.

Before retiring for the day, I tried to call Don Welsh to determine if he was coming out that weekend. I left a message on his machine. He had probably taken another trip abroad. He just can't stay away from those freebie rides that came with airline retirement. Several people had asked about him at the party; we missed not having him there.

Also, almost everyone asked about Jackie and whether she was coming to the Fly-In over the weekend. I found it hard to answer with any certainty, so I just said, "Well, maybe tomorrow." I had sure hoped so.

I called home at nine PM as usual. Everyone was in good spirits and I went to great length to describe my day and tried to help them enjoy the party and all the festivities vicariously. I missed them.

A decision to turn in early came easy. It had been a long three days since leaving Maryland. I was finally relaxed and looking forward to a great fun day tomorrow and, hopefully, calmer winds.

# CHAPTER 37

## *SATURDAY—DAY FOUR*

**WAKING UP SATURDAY** morning to the hissing sound of a hot air balloon propane burner going over the top of the motel and "Dusty Farmer Restaurant," I knew it had to be a reasonably calm morning. Next, I heard the familiar growl of a round engine and knew a Stearman was flying and that I had overslept.

It was now seven thirty a.m. and an hour later than I had planned to be in bed. I slowly dragged myself out of bed, showered and headed to the airport for some sausage, eggs, and pancakes, and about a gallon of cowboy coffee. For good cowboy coffee, according to my Dad, the best ratio of coffee to water is one handful of coffee to a cupful of water. I do plan to give up this addiction someday. (In my next lifetime.)

Hot air balloon pilots usually start showing up around four a.m. Shortly thereafter, they start unloading their trailers, and by daybreak they have the balloons unloaded, rolled out, and filled with air.

I observed this early morning ritual while sleeping under the wings of my Stearman the first two years here. Feeling safe and secure in my cocoon, I could usually sleep through most of the activity—up until they started the fans that initially fill the balloons. And then the yelling of orders over the fan noise would elevate me straight up in my sleeping bag. I moved into a motel the third year.

One year, sometime after midnight, while Steve Dubois and I were sleeping under the wings, a thunderstorm moved through the area. To stay dry I had moved under the wide space between the landing gear and behind the engine. I smelled gas from time to time, but didn't realize it was my sleeping bag getting saturated from a small fuel drip coming from the engine area. The balloonist that woke me up early that morning never realized he had probably saved me from death by asphyxiation.

Several people do sleep under the wings every year at the Fly-In. Some of them even sleep in tents under the higher winged planes. Jim Walters and his son usually pitched their tent between our planes to escape the Kansas wind and creatures of the night. Year after year a few of these hardy souls continue to brave the elements of weather, the nuisance of noise, and reports of rattlesnakes nearby.

I've only seen one snake there in the past fifteen years. It was a non-poisonous bull snake, which resembles the rattlesnake at first appearance. Don had startled it from where it had been sleeping in one of the half tires cut and placed around a tie-down chain. Don jumped back when it started crawling out of the tire. I yelled, "Snake!" and people skedaddled in all directions away from the Stearman. Its presence alone caused much excitement and lots of Indian war dancing by almost everyone within twenty feet of the plane.

# CHAPTER 38

**BY THE TIME** I got to the airport, the clear blue north-ern horizon was filled with various sizes, shapes, and colors of hot air balloons. Two Stearmans were flying in formation across the middle of the field with smoke trails while several others were being warmed up for flight. A group of skydivers were huddled in a circle practicing their in-flight maneuvers next to the jump plane. A large crowd of people had already gathered at the pancake and sausage breakfast held in one of the hangers. This was the making of another great St. Francis Stearman Fly-In.

After removing the engine and cockpit cov-ers, I was very pleased to find that the engine was no longer leaking oil. I think Le Beast likes the dry Kansas climate. It was a little dusty and dirty, but I knew it would be a few days before I could wash it thoroughly. Until then I would continue applying spray polish to keep most of the bugs and dust removed.

While doing a preflight inspection of the cockpit, I decided to turn on the GPS and run it through a complete global position fix. I knew this would take about forty-five minutes to accomplish, so I left it on and went to breakfast.

Also, since I wanted to stay in the year 1928 for the weekend, I decided not to wind the clock until I was ready to leave.

After a hardy breakfast, I filled the plane with gas and oil, and then cleaned both windshields. By this time the GPS had finished its global position fix. I requested its present position and it informed me that it had just arrived in St. Francis, Kansas. I sighed and said, "Thanks a lot, you worthless piece of crap." Later, I reluctantly charged the standby battery and tested it again over the weekend, but I still didn't completely trust it.

# CHAPTER 39

**MOST BIPLANE FLY-INS** attract a variety of classic and older aircraft besides Stearmans. At any point in time over the weekend, several war birds, as well as pre-war and post-war planes, would stop by to join the activity. We are very fortunate that a large number of war-birds and WWII pilots continue to show up here every year.

This weekend would be no exception. Three American T6's, a D18 Beech, a T-28, two Cessna 195s, a 450 Ag Cat, and a 1927 Eaglerock were but a few of the round engine airplanes stopping here today. Hopefully, most of these birds will still be flying in another fifty years.

Eventually, over the three-day period, there would be an assortment of flying machines here. They would range from slow-speed ultra-lights to high-speed turboprop twins. The idea being "everyone is welcome here."

In this farm country, all types of friendly people start showing up early. From sunrise to sunset they drift by to participate in the great experience of barnstorming. They come here to witness daredevil stunts; ride in classic WWII biplanes, fly in hot air balloons, skydive from planes, share war stories, eat good food, and to observe the bikini-clad ladies sunbathing next to the skydiving hanger. It's all good, clean, Kansas fun!

By mid-day most of the balloonists had returned to the airport with their baskets, canopies, and unopened bottles of champagne securely stored away in various trailer compartments. They would have a few new war-stories to share with everyone. For weeks to come their passengers would relive, over and over, all the excitement and wonder of floating peacefully over the Kansas farmland.

For several years I have enjoyed taking one particular balloon pilot for a Stearman ride. He's as big as a football player, but he seems to be laid back and easygoing. We both enjoy doing hammerhead stalls and barrel rolls. This year his daughter bought him a ride for father's day. I have an open invitation to go up with him any morning I want to get up at four thirty a.m. I'm certain I will accept his offer eventually. Hey, if it flies and it looks like fun, what else is there to consider? Just time and opportunity, that's all.

# CHAPTER 40

**BY NOON THE** sun was high overhead and the prairie landscape was awash with full color. A long Kansas summer was starting to bloom and the forecasted ninety-three degrees was just the beginning. The excited crowd was almost at a peak and there was a line of people waiting for rides. A large number of jumpers were either in the air or jockeying around in a circle waiting on the plane to land for a ride upstairs. The hot dog stand and tee shirt concessions were booming with business. A couple of airplanes were lined up waiting to refuel at the pump area. It was a hustling, bustling, real live Fly-In.

It's great fun just watching the people during a ride and seeing how their expressions change over a short period of time. At first they're hesitant about the whole idea of riding in an old wood and fabric plane. Then, after watching the first survivors, they finally decide to give it a try. I talk to my passengers through the intercom to help them relax and I tell them about the history of the Stearman. I watch their expressions through a two-way mirror under the upper wing and try to smile a lot. Their faces gradually change from reservation to enjoyment, then to sheer delight or absolute ecstasy in less than twenty minutes. I never grow tired of seeing this wonderful transformation.

Each year there seems to be one passenger that you remember more than the rest. This year it was a ten- or eleven-year-old lad named Tommy, wearing a bright green John Deere baseball cap.

He kept shifting from one leg to the other, hanging around and watching everything with wide-eyed amazement. After absorbing everything in sight he finally worked up enough courage to come over to the plane.

"Hey mister, are you giving rides?"

I replied, "Yes, we're selling rides."

He asked how much, and I told him, "Forty dollars to cover expenses."

"But I don't have forty dollars."

"Well, you'll need to have your parents stop by to see me after lunch and I'll try to work something out with them." I needed their permission to take him for a ride more than I needed the forty dollars.

Before I left the airport property he was back again. He couldn't find his parents, but he wanted to watch my plane for me while I went to lunch. I said, "Okay, just make sure that nobody climbs on the wings and I'll give you a couple of bucks when I get back." He smiled and took off towards Le Beast for guard duty.

After swapping a few war-stories over lunch with some fellow Stearman pilots, we discussed the issue of liability and rides. Each of them had their own horror story about insurance, lawyers, and liability. One pilot had lost his airplane to a teenager who froze up on the controls causing him to almost corkscrew into the ground. Another had been held up in court for years when the parents of a ten-year-old decided to sue him for causing psychological problems caused by a crash landing. They were all in agreement that flying a minor without parental consent was more risk than they were willing to take. By the time we finished lunch, I was inclined to agree with their opinions.

While walking back across the road to the airport, I hoped Tommy had found his parents. He was walking around the plane with the strut of a British Royal Guardsman and the alertness of a Fort Knox security guard (but without a gun). He reported that he had chased several would-be Stearman destroying maniacs away from the plane in my absence. I paid him two dollars, as promised, and another dollar for the report.

He asked if three dollars would buy a short ride and I said, "Maybe, but I still need to talk to your folks first." I suggested that he go to lunch and then try to find his parents. He kicked at the grass and left for the terminal with his head held down. Again, I hoped he would find them.

I am always amazed by the variety of people who buy biplane rides. They come in all shapes, sizes and ages. Each with varying expectations and reservations about this whole adventure, they come from near and far to experience this thing called barnstorming.

That day alone, I gave a ride to an eighty-year-old man who had never flown and a thirty-year-old female airline pilot with two thousand hours flying time. Also, I flew with a huge linebacker who blocked out my forward vision, and a shapely young lady who can come back and block my vision for free anytime she desires.

They all come for different reasons, but they leave with something in common. They have each experienced the wind and the sun in their face and smelled the sweet warm aroma of smoke from a round engine. They usually have a smile on their face when the leave, and most of them will have pleasant memories that stay awhile. They might forget the name of the pilot that flew them, but they will never forget their first Stearman ride.

After giving a few more rides, I met Tommy with an updated report on the missing parents. They had gone to visit an aunt in town, and they would pick him and his friends up there later. Also, they would not be coming back to the airport, and they also didn't have forty dollars for a ride. He kicked at the grass again and said, "So, I guess I can't take a ride today, huh?"

Hoping to satisfy his desire to fly I said, "Maybe I can let you taxi with me over to the gas pit since I need to refuel."

He lit up like a Christmas tree at this suggestion and said, "Okay, cool!"

I helped him into the front cockpit and strapped him down tight with the seat belts. At first I wasn't sure I could get the cloth helmet snapped together with that large smile he had on his face, but then he relaxed and started with the questions. "How does this work? How does that work? What does this do? Etc., etc., etc." Actually, he was asking all the right questions that any student pilot would ask.

He stayed in the cockpit during refueling. With the control stick in hand he flew thousands of miles, I'm sure. I took a longer route back to the tie-down area. Taxiing fast around the triangle of the runways, I occasionally lifted the tail wheel off the ground so he could get a feel of flying. He held his head over the side around the windshield to feel the wind in his face. He never had a thought that didn't cross his lips on the way back in. We never left the ground, but he thought we had.

When we got back, I asked him how he liked, and he thought it was "Grrreat!" He thanked me profusely before he bolted towards the terminal to share this great adventure with his friends. I grinned to myself thinking that I had just pulled the wool over Tommy's eyes.

Throughout the afternoon I noticed him talking to several other Stearman pilots and pointing towards me. I felt sure he was trying to hustle another ride, but there were no other takers. He hung around the airport most of the afternoon and came back to share the rest of his life's story with me and to guard Le Beast occasionally while I was away on breaks.

Later in the day, when I went for fuel, he was right there and begging with his eyes for one last ride. During another long, fast taxi back to the tie-down area, he asked, "What's it like to fly up there with the hawks and where the other airplanes are flying?"

At that point I already had the tail wheel off the ground. I thought to myself, *To hell with it all, I'm gonna take this kid for a ride.* After increasing to full power, Le Beast gently lifted us from the grass and slowly carried us around the airport pattern. He kept looking up at the clouds and down at the ground in star-eyed wonder. He waved at the other planes and everything else he saw, including cars and people on the ground. For the first time that day he didn't have anything to say. His smile kept getting in the way.

After landing, all he could say was, "I flew, I flew, I flew."

He thanked me over and over again and, then he disappeared into a circle of friends waiting at the terminal. I never saw him again. Little Tommy was gone. I hope to see him again next year—hopefully, with his parents.

# CHAPTER 41

**AROUND TWO PM,** the big event for the Stearman pilots is the balloon burst and spot-landing contest. A ground crew releases helium balloons and each pilot has a chance to spot and burst three balloons in the air with their propellers. In case of a tie, the winner is determined with the best spot landing across a white chalk line.

Regardless of who takes first place, there's always that quasi-serious bantering between rivals before is starts. It's all good-natured fun, but we try to psyche each other with comments like "Are you feeling OK today?" or "Man, that engine on your plane seems to be running a little rough."

I kept hoping to see Jackie, but she didn't show up and it almost broke my heart. I deserved it; I should have called her. Since she wasn't there, I asked Steve Dubois to ride shotgun for me and to help spot the balloons. In sharing my technique with him I became too involved in the process and missed two out of three for the first time ever.

As it turned out, Eric burst the most balloons and won the contest, but I'm sure my spot landing was better. He would gloat and brag for rest of the day and part of the night—typical winner attitude. I should know.

I'm reasonably sure the skydivers and balloonist have similar contests and probably have just as much fun as we do. Especially with spot landings. I haven't watched the hot air balloons land, but it appears that the skydivers are always trying to land on a specified spot. I've never tried skydiving and never had a balloon ride. Just gotta do that someday.

Every year we seem to have some type of media coverage for the Fly-In. One year it might be a newspaper and the next year it could be a radio or TV station. We take it all in stride and try to share the experience with as many people as possible.

One year the Smithsonian Air and Space magazine did a story on the Stearman and came to St. Francis for interviews and photos. Robert Grace, Eric Baldwin, and I did the flying for the pictures, while Don Welsh conducted most of the interview from the ground.

When I got my copy of the magazine a few months later, it included quite a few pictures of our planes, but only one picture of a pilot—Don Welsh. Needless to say, Don had a heyday with that situation for a while. I gave Don a copy, but only after I harassed him about his new found celebrity. I eventually got his autograph and I still have that copy of the magazine. I plan to keep it.

After installing the engine and canopy covers and tying the plane down for the day, I walked up and down the flight line and talked to the other biplane pilots. Everyone had had a great time and had given quite a few rides. A big red Stearman had just landed and would be taxiing up with his last passenger of the day. It was Eric, of course. The crowd has thinned down to only a handful of dedicated visitors.

Two things caught my eye as we left the airport. Off in the distance I saw the build-up of a large thunderstorm in the south. I hoped it was just a daily storm and not the edge of the low-pressure front that was slowly overtaking the high-pressure system we were enjoying. I had planned to leave tomorrow in time to stay ahead of the front and maybe have a tailwind on my return trip. The second thing I noticed was a group of skydivers loading up in a twin-engine jump plane. Their last jump for the day would be into the City Park for the barbecue picnic.

# CHAPTER 42

**WITHOUT A DOUBT,** the best barbeque beef in the world can be found in St. Francis, Kansas, at the Stearman Fly-In. I don't know if they prepare this outstanding treat any other time of the year, but I do know it's the best beef I've ever eaten in my lifetime.

They barbecue the beef on a smoker-type grill that resembles a fifty-five-gallon drum cut in half, on wheels, and with a smokestack on one end. This shredded beef, served on a bun with a mild homemade sauce, always keeps me begging for more. Along with the beef, a table full of potatoes, coleslaw, baked beans, and iced tea are there for the asking. They even serve homemade ice cream. The atmosphere is more like a Fourth of July celebration instead of a town picnic.

After the barbecue Robert Grace does the official "Welcome to the St. Francis Fly-In" for those in attendance. He always takes time to thank all the good people who help make this event possible each year. He talked about the activities taking place and then handed out the awards for the contests. Eric tried to be all gracious and humble when he accepted the award for bursting the most balloons. He was almost convincing.

Afterwards there's usually some type of entertainment. Over the years we've seen a variety of local talent including singers, dancers, and musicians. One year, a few of the younger ladies began line dancing on the grass while a very young fellow with a large cowboy hat sang his version of "Boot Scoot Boogie." Mel even gave it a try. It was such great fun to watch.

Before calling it a day, we stopped by the airport to check on the airplanes one last time. It seems to be a ritual with most of the pilots. We talk about the things we experienced that day and what the battle plan was for tomorrow. Pilot bonding stuff.

I talked about the young boy Tommy who finally got his ride. The pilots I had lunch with just shook their heads, but I told them I thought it was the right thing to do. Someone suggested it was something John Grace would have done. We all fell silent and nodded our heads in agreement.

Everyone hated to see the day end, but we slowly drifted away from the planes and headed for the motel or our sleeping bags. It had been another beautiful day in paradise.

The last thing before hitting the sack was to call home and check on things. Mel said she still hadn't completely forgiven me for not bringing her on the trip. I knew that she would eventually forgive me, but it bothered me a lot to know that I had two daughters who were not too pleased with me at the same time. I felt like a rat.

I told them about the great time I was having. They said they were also having a good vacation. Especially without me hanging around with my head down, bitching and griping about not being able to go to St. Francis "again" this year. I told them I missed them, too.

# CHAPTER 43

## *SUNDAY—DAY FIVE*

**SUNDAY MORNING, THE** hot air balloons and early Stearman fliers were flying low over the motel, waking everyone up again. Knowing that I would probably be leaving later in the day for Concordia, I had planned to sleep in for an extra hour or so. But I woke up and immediately had a desperate craving for some more cowboy coffee. So I stumbled out of bed and followed my nose to the airport for another pancake and sausage breakfast around eight a.m.

By the time I got to the airport, most everyone was getting geared up for another day of sun and fun. The balloons were already up and the skydivers were getting ready to load up.

Aside from rides, the major Stearman activity for today would be the mid-morning formation flyover. It takes a lot of coordination and trust in your fellow pilot's skill to make this maneuver safe and successful. We always select a lead pilot with the level of experience and training that's needed to pull it all together. We were all glad there would not be a "missing man" formation again this year. The last one we did was for John Grace a few years ago.

I decided to pass on the formation flyover and get ready for the long afternoon trip instead. A check on the weather told me I needed to leave by noon to stay ahead of the frontal activity coming up from the south. A large low-pressure system was continuing to develop and it would replace the clear VFR conditions we had enjoyed over the weekend. Hopefully, the farmers would get some desperately needed rain over the next few days.

Several Colorado friends showed up and I managed to give a few rides. Roger Koenig, the previous owner of my first Stearman, and his family from Yuma were all there. After he checked me out in the Stearman we became good friends and shared a lot of flying together over the years. It was great to see them again.

My friend and fellow spray pilot, Craig Michael, hinted that if I hung around he just might put me to work—again—spraying in Yuma County for the rest of the season. We had sprayed several thousand acres of wheat over the years, and I was tempted, but I knew I had to get back to Maryland soon. I declined several invitations to stay over for a few days, but I wished my schedule had been such that I could have accepted all their generous offers. Maybe next time.

Steve Dubois graciously extended an invitation to fly his new Stearman and I enthusiastically accepted. It took him twenty years to rebuild it from the ground up, and it's a beauty. It was an honor and privilege I could not refuse. Most Stearman pilots will never let anyone fly their planes regardless of your experience. I miss not having Steve around to fly with and to help me when I have a problem with Le Beast. He's a good friend and one of the finest wood and fabric craftsmen and round engine mechanics I've ever known.

# CHAPTER 44

**BY NOON MOST** of the activity had slowed down, all except the skydivers. They kept going all day like battery-powered bunnies. It sure looks like a lot of fun. Every time I think about it I just know that I'll eventually get up enough nerve to jump some-day. Perhaps next year.

While charging the batteries, I checked out of the motel, packed the plane, and then hung around talking to other pilots and friends until around two p.m. It was hard to leave again. But finally it was time to yell, "Clear prop! Concordia, here I come." I wound the eight-day clock ten times to get a jump-start on my journey forward in time.

After takeoff, I circled the field and made a final pass with the smoker going full blast and waved to the small remaining crowd. I decided to make one final circle over John Grace's gravesite before heading east. As I flew away from the graveyard, I still remained puzzled about this mysterious influence that had brought me back to St. Francis. And why wasn't Jackie there? When would I see her again?

Somewhere between Bird City and Norton I saw the 1928 Ford Roadster again driving east on Highway 36, and I circled around to wave at the driver. It was a man with a gray beard wearing a baseball cap.

Then, slowly but surely, we pulled away from the roadster, the man, and the year 1928.

# PART IV

## - HOMEWARD BOUND -

# CHAPTER 45

*Flying across the Heartland in a 50-year-old biplane; feeling the warm sun and wind on your face; smelling the sweet aroma of smoke from a radial engine; absorbing the oceans of unending farmland lying below you. This must be heaven; no other experience on earth even comes close.*

**Somewhere over Kansas in June.**

**DURING THE FIRST** hour of flight there was a steady southwest tailwind that significantly increased my ground speed. At first I began feeling quite smug about my wind prediction and just knew that Mother Nature was indeed predictable after all.

Then, passing by Norton airport, I noticed the windsock was moving in a south-southeast direction. The quartering tailwind had just become an intermittent quartering headwind. I had waited a little too long before leaving St. Francis to stay ahead of the frontal winds. This system was developing faster than I had expected. The afterglow of the weekend helped me shrug my shoulders and say, "Oh well."

With an unpredictable headwind, I decided to make a fuel stop at the Phillipsburg airport and take a short break. I have a two-hour fuel tank in the plane, but only a one-hour bladder. I guess I drank too much cowboy coffee before leaving St. Francis.

Phillipsburg has a nice airport and the attendant was a spray pilot (of course). I was beginning to think spray pilots ran most of the airports in western Kansas. Maybe they do. He echoed what Robert Grace had shared with me Friday about the dry spraying season, but I knew these hardy Americans would find a way to tough it out. They always do.

Heading towards Concordia, I decided to keep flying for a while and trying to get back ahead of the frontal system winds. I thought I still had plenty of time to make it back to Cameron, Missouri, before dark. I knew I could get the plane inside for the night if I could get there before they closed for the day. I wondered how long it would take to drive from Cameron to Jackie's house in Kansas City.

A ground speed check, after the first hour, told me I would need to make another fuel stop before reaching Cameron airport. After a quick check of the chart I decided my next landing would be at

Marysville, Kansas. I hoped there would be some-one there on a Sunday afternoon to sell me the fuel I needed.

Upon landing, I found the airport vacant as King Tut's tomb. No gas pump and nobody home. The small modular terminal building had a soda machine and a telephone inside, but no directory. At first I thought about flying on to Hiawatha, but I wasn't sure I would find the local spray pilot there on a late Sunday afternoon either. (Yes, another spray pilot operates the local airport there.)

While walking around the airport to confirm that I was there alone, I discovered that the busi-ness office was also locked. However, I could see the coffee machine through the front window; could almost smell it through the glass. But since I didn't want to go to jail for breaking and entering, I started walking back towards the terminal.

A car was pulling up as I walked back to the plane. It was a young lady with two dogs. I explained my situation to her and she gave me the name of one of the pilots based there.

I got the phone number from the operator and called his home. His wife said he was in town, but she felt sure he could help when he returned. About twenty minutes later Ron was refueling Le Beast.

As he got out of his truck he looked at Le Beast and said, "Nice Stearman. Where you been, St. Francis?"

"Thanks. Yeah, I spent all weekend there."

"Where you headed?"

"Back to Maryland, but I need enough fuel to get me to Cameron, Missouri, before dark. Sorry to get you out on your day off."

"It's not a problem at all. If we don't help each other in general aviation today, we'll never survive," he said as he unlocked the fuel shed.

I knew he was right, but still felt bad about disturbing him on a Sunday. Those friendly Kansas folks are great people. I was in such a hurry that I forgot to ask him if he was a spray pilot.

Before leaving I called Steve Cox at the Cameron airport. He said they were just leaving for the day and wouldn't be there when I arrived. They would not be able to put the plane inside; however, I was welcome to tie it down for the night in front of the larger hanger. Also, he gave me the phone number for a local cab company and instructions on how to operate the fuel system in case I wanted to leave early in the morning.

It was getting late in the day and I had not eaten since breakfast, so it was time to raid the old flight bag again for an energy bar. I washed it down with a Dr. Pepper and then it was time to clear prop again.

# CHAPTER 46

**ON THE WAY** out of Kansas I flew around the grave-yard at Hiawatha with the smoker on and waived to the relatives again. Shortly thereafter, I crossed over the Missouri River and immediately started noticing storm clouds on the horizon moving up from the south. I was beginning to believe that this basin area was creating its own weather system.

The weather was starting to close in around us the closer we got to Cameron. I kept checking for a clear path behind us for a quick 180 degree turn if needed. However, I was starting to have doubts about reaching the Cameron Airport at that point. I thought to myself, *Probably should have stopped in Concordia after all; maybe called Jackie from there.*

I had worked my way south going around the St. Joseph area and was trying to gradually work my way back north. There were several storm cells around, with lightning bolts at the cloud base and dark streamers of heavy rain falling earthward. It was getting late in the day and the sun had all but disappeared behind the clouds. I tightened my seat belt and said aloud, "Looks like you're in for another wild ride, cowboy. Just like the takeoff at Norton airport last week—if not worse."

Working my way back south again to get around a rather ominous-looking cell, I suddenly found myself completely surrounded by thunder, lightning, strong updrafts, heavy rain, and an ink-black wall about a mile straight ahead. I held my hands and feet on the controls with a light but firm grip. We suddenly shifted sideways about forty-five degrees to the left and, for what seemed a lifetime, we slammed up and down with teeth-rattling jolts. Then we shifted sideways to the right and the rain howled into the cockpit and blew my goggles up to my forehead.

Without a clear horizon for reference, it was hard to tell if we were climbing, diving, rolling or spinning. I continued to hold the stick and rudder pedals with a firm but loose grip. Trying to over-control the plane could only make the situation worse. I looked outside the cockpit to the right and left, then finally saw my left wing was at about a sixty-degree angle to the ground, with the nose tilted downward. Slowly but deliberately I did a shallow right turn and brought the plane back to level flight, as the hair on the back of my neck began to stick out like porcupine quills. My first inclination was to do a one-hundred-eighty-degree turn and get the hell out of there, a.s.a.p.

A quick look over my shoulder told me that was no longer an option. Scolding myself and shaking my head I shouted, "Oh boy, Russ, you've done it this time!" In a nanosecond I knew I had to get closer to the ground for better reference.

I was quickly reminded of a trip I had taken across the Delaware Bay in a Super Cub, when I got caught in low hanging clouds. We had to fly a few feet above the surface of the water in order to know which was up. We were lucky we didn't wind up in the middle of the Atlantic Ocean and out of fuel. As a private pilot with seventy-five hours flying time I didn't know any better at the time.

As a commercial pilot with over five thousand hours flying time it was just plain dumb to be caught in this situation. I knew that without proper instruments in the plane I had to get down out of the clouds where I could use the ground as a level reference point.

Looking straight ahead I saw a clearing and a patch of earth below, so I pulled the throttle back to 1500 rpm in order to maintain a slower speed, then trimmed the plane to 74 mph and headed for the ground. While keeping an eye on the altimeter, airspeed, and compass, I started a slow descent around the dark rolling clouds. The altimeter went from 1000 feet to 900, then 800, then 750, 800, 1000, and back to 800; the airspeed went from 80 mph to 95, then 100, 75, 65, and 80; and the compass read 45 degrees, then 50, 60, 70, 50, 35, 25, and 20. We had descended into the edge of a storm cell and were turning to the left.

I slowly added a little right rudder until we were back to 50 degrees again, and held on.

Eons of time passed as we gradually jolted, rattled, and bumped our way back and forth, up and down, and I was slammed around in the cockpit like a steel ball in a pinball machine. My goggles flew off again, but I didn't dare take my hands off the controls to replace them. A flood of rain was washing over and around the windshield like Niagara Falls, as the dark clouds consumed us and the sky turned into an inferno of lightening.

"What a dumbass, what a dumbass," was all I could say.

After another lifetime of bone-jolting we gradually cleared the clouds, but the ominous jet-black wall of other clouds was only a quarter mile ahead. If I had been wearing a parachute, I do believe I would have jumped at that point. I had "Stayed with the plan," and, in doing so, I had just run out of options.

Then, from out of nowhere, I saw what had to be the most beautiful and brightest rainbow I've ever seen in my lifetime. It was at the base of the black wall and I could see the ground beneath its brilliant arch. The closer I got, the more I was drawn into its radiant beauty. I found myself completely mesmerized by the pulsing light and I knew I had no choice but to pass under the rainbow.

My last thought before entering was that if I closed my eyes I would somehow pass through this corridor and reach some other, safer period of time. I was so completely hypnotized, and everything was happening in such slow motion, that I completely surrendered to its effect and thought aloud, "Maybe this is where I'll find the answer to why I came on this trip."

# CHAPTER 47

**PASSING UNDER THE** rainbow was an indescrib-
able, almost surreal, out-of-body experience at
first. We entered a deafening cone of silence that
completely engulfed both man and machine,
and we found ourselves suspended like peaceful
figures in a snow globe as we floated lazily across
a beautiful lush Missouri landscape.

An ocean of color inside of the rainbow slowly
changed from bright red to orange red, then we
moved into a complete spectrum of violet colors as its arch gently pulsated above a soft white
misty fog. I closed my eyes for a moment as we
drifted under the brilliance of ever-changing light
and hoped that we would stay there for a while.

But it faded almost as soon as it appeared, and
then Cameron Airport appeared through the rain
on the nose of the plane. Still dazed by this experienced, I made a gentle turn over the field then

slowly turned to a descending final approach and came floating back to the earth.

Shortly thereafter I suddenly realized I was still flying and had a handful of Stearman hydroplaning down a wet runway with half of it already behind me. It didn't take me long to snap out of the daydream and gradually brake to a stop about one hundred yards from the end of the pavement.

After I stopped, I sat there a few minutes to gather my thoughts and tried to understand what had just happened. Then, it started to rain and I was getting wet. The only way to keep rain out of the cockpit on the ground is to keep the airplane moving.

Taxiing east towards the terminal, I looked over my shoulder to see the rainbow again, but it was gone. The jet-black wall had closed the opening and a wall of rain was bearing down on the airport.

# CHAPTER 48

**TAXIING AROUND THE** airport and looking for an open hanger to get out of the rain, I soon realized there was none to be found. A tie-down area in front of the main hanger was where we would have to weather out the storm.

I hurried out of the plane to get the tail wheel tied down since it was pointed into the oncoming wind. The tie-down rope for the tail was in a lower grassy spot and the main wheels were on higher pavement. I pulled the cockpit cover out of the baggage compartment and strapped it over the windshields just before I draped the engine cover over my head and headed for cover under the fuselage between the main gears. Then it *really* started to rain.

The driving wind and drenching monsoon rain lasted for at least forty-five minutes before it finally began to let up. I remained somewhat dry there beneath the plane, except when the wind decided to blow sideways.

At first the rain felt cool and refreshing to Le Beast and myself after being in the hot sun for three days, but after watching the Kansas dust wash off the wings for an hour we were more than amply refreshed. And Mother Nature had just kicked my ass good and was starting to get on my bad side again.

While sitting there beneath the plane I thought about the John Grace dream, the storm, the trip, the family back home, and Jackie. I had really missed not having her in my life and not seeing her at the Fly-In this year. I had wanted her to fly out with me, but we had both been too damn stubborn with pride to call each other ahead of time. Since she lived only eighty miles south of Cameron I thought this might be the place and time to call her and try to patch up our differences. I was tired and hungry and still needed to find a motel for the night, so I decided to wait until tomorrow to make the decision to call or not.

While waiting on a cab I noticed another small rainbow on the horizon in front of another black wall off to the south. It glowed brightly for only a few seconds, but it was enough of an omen to convince me that I needed to call her in the morning.

# CHAPTER 49

## *MONDAY—DAY SIX*

**IT WAS STILL** overcast and raining when I woke up Monday morning. A call to flight services confirmed what I had already suspected: the front had moved through overnight and was halfway across Missouri. This meant that I would be on the backside of the clear high-pressure system and into a wet low-pressure system for the next few days.

After my second cup of caffeine from the motel coffee machine, I paced back and forth across the room like a caged tiger. The time had arrived when I finally had to call Jackie or walk away from what was probably the last chance to settle our differences. I picked up and put down the phone several times before finally dialing her number at seven a.m.

"Hello…Helloo, this is Jackie, who's there?"

My heart was pounding and I couldn't find my voice at first. Finally I said, "Hey, kid, this is your Dad, don't hang up, okay?"

"Okay. Is everything all right?"

"Yeah, everything's fine."

"Where are you?"

"I'm in Cameron. Just called to see if you might want to drive up and meet me at the airport. I think it's time we had a little talk, don't you?"

"Yeah, maybe. You're at the airport? What are you doing at the airport?"

"Well, I'm on my way home. Been to St. Francis for the Fly-In and got caught here in the storms last night."

She didn't respond at first, but finally said, "Oh, is that right? Well, let me make a few calls and I think I can be there around eleven. If that's okay?" Her voice had suddenly grown distant.

"That's fine. The weather has me grounded here for a while anyway. I'll see you around eleven or so."

She said, "Okay, eleven sharp!" Then with a "click" she was gone again before I could respond.

I probably shouldn't have mentioned St. Francis until she got here. But, hey, I'm just a man, what do I know?

After a leisurely breakfast that lasted until nine-thirty, it was time to meet Steve Cox at the Cameron airport again. He was very apologetic about not being able to get the plane into a hanger overnight.

I jokingly suggested, "We both needed a good bath to wash away the Kansas dust we had accumulated from the Fly-In at St. Francis over the weekend," and Steve and I both laughed. Then we discussed the frontal system and I told him I planned to leave by midafternoon if the weather cleared. Obviously, he had some doubts about flying anywhere that day since he had already cancelled most of student activity he had scheduled.

He said, "The rain gauge showed we got three inches of rain overnight."

I told him, "It felt more like three feet."

The Stearman didn't have any more Kansas dust on it, and most of the wax I had recently applied had also washed off overnight.

While hanging around the office and nervously waiting on Jackie, I noticed Steve had several GPS units displayed for sale. He carefully explained all the great and wonderful capabilities of these state-of-the-art receivers and he almost had me convinced to update my panel on the spot. I asked about trade-ins and he tried not to laugh when I gave him the make and model of the unit already in the plane. He said there just wasn't a large resale demand for that "Fine piece of navigation equipment with outstanding qualities" that I had described, so I decided to wait.

I had turned the GPS on a few times while coming in from Kansas yesterday, and it seemed to be working okay, but I had not relied on it continuously. What I had relied on was my finger on the map—at least until I flew under the rainbow.

# CHAPTER 50

**WHILE NERVOUSLY WAITING** on Jackie, I took the covers off the engine and cockpits and opened the baggage compartment and a few panels to help dry out the plane. I draped the covers and my flying jacket over the airport security fence to dry them out and walked over to untie the plane. I looked up to see her pulling up in a sleek red Mustang Cobra just outside the airport fence. She was right on schedule—as usual. A steel band immediately tightened around my chest. Trying to talk myself into composure, I waved to her as she was passing the fence gate.

"Hey kid! Would you bring my flying jacket?"

In one quick motion she gave me a salute and tossed the jacket over her shoulder.

Fathers always find it hard to think of their little girls as being all grown up, but that was the day I finally had to face reality. This was a woman, not a child. Watching her swagger across the airport apron, dressed in jeans and a tan shirt with my flying jacket draped across one shoulder, I was transported back in time. With her aviation glasses pushed up onto her head and a look of determination (with a touch of her fathers' arrogance), she looked similar to a WWII WAC (Women's Army Corps) pilot getting ready for another ferrying mission.

The closer she got the deeper my heart sank in my chest, and I suddenly realized that I had a lump in my throat. I walked towards her and opened my arms. We held each other loosely and I spoke very slowly and softly.

"Don't say anything, sweetheart. Don't say a word. Just listen to me for a minute. I am your father and I love you, that's all we need to say for now."

I felt her relax and put her head on my shoulder. "I love you too, Dad."

Then we held each other tightly and we both cried.

Shortly thereafter, we began to nervously chat about the trip and St. Francis. The first thing she asked was "Who won the balloon burst and spot landing contest?" When I told her that Eric won, she laughed and said, "Well, it had to happen someday, maybe you're slipping a little now that you're a few years older."

"What do you mean 'slipping?' I'm just a little rusty from not being there the past two years, that's all."

"If I remember correctly, the last time we flew there you burst thirteen balloons. And the year before that I did my first jump while you did ten balloons."

Then we laughed. We both have a way of bringing back only the best of memories. After a while we decided to go to lunch in town so we could drink our share of local coffee and eventually talk about other things.

# CHAPTER 51

**WE WERE AHEAD** of the lunch crowd so we sat down in the small art-deco restaurant with red checkered tablecloths. The waitress, dressed in a '50s style poodle skirt, white Bobbie socks, and sneakers, waited for us to decide where we wanted to sit. We were in luck. We both spotted a booth by a window. It appeared to be the only quiet corner space in the restaurant. The waitress handed us menus and asked, "Would you guys like something to drink?"

Almost in unison we both asked, "Do you have Colombian Coffee?" We both smiled.

The waitress looked back and forth at us then said, "Let me guess, father and daughter, right?"

We both nodded our heads and I replied, "Yep." Jackie added, "You bet."

Over lunch we talked of this and that. Still trying to act like nothing had ever happened, but feeling the air of tension building between us. We ran out of small talk so I started talking about St. Francis and the Stearman again.

Jackie looked up at me and said, "Wait a minute Dad." I started to say something else, but she held up her hand. "No, I want you to listen to me first, okay?"

I let her sit back for a minute, obviously collecting her thoughts. She wanted to "cut to the chase" of things.

"These past two years we will never get back, you know that and I know that. What we choose to do now is to either accept one another for who we are, or I can get in my car and drive away."

"Okay," I replied. "Talk to me."

She turned and looked out the window. "Not to make light of the way I acted or to make excuses for the things I said, but you didn't realize that there was a lot going on with me and I was needing you—NOT for the Cub. I needed you to just be there as a friend and a father."

The waitress came by and asked if we needed more coffee, but sensing her presence was not wanted, quickly slipped away with pot in hand.

"God, Dad, we are so much alike. You don't want to open up and you're so stubborn and selfish and I am the same damn way. Rather than saying I needed you, I had to act like a spoiled child not getting her way about some stupid airplane."

"Sweetheart, I know how important that plane was and how much you wanted me to work on it."

She cut me off immediately. "Dad, please listen to what I am saying. All of it. None of it was ever, ever about the plane. It was about the times that I needed you and felt like you weren't there. Especially in my teens and early twenties." Tears started to well up in her eyes. "I'm getting a divorce, Dad. It has been a while coming, but there it is. I wanted so much to ask you for advice, but was at a stage in my life where instead of accepting that we are who we are, I instead chose to just be bitter and resentful. I completely turned everything, absolutely everything around to be about you and your shortcomings. I stretched out everything you had ever done, real or imagined, and tried to hurt you with it. I did this as a way of coping and not having to look inside myself for answers."

She bowed her head and softly said, "But I need you now and I am so tired of being sad. I am so tired of waking up and being angry at the world for not giving me what I wanted. I never looked at how much the world has already given me, and I never considered how much you still have to give me. I only looked at what I thought I hadn't received."

She finally looked at me and I could tell it was all she could do to keep her composure. "I love you, Dad. Not in spite of the things you are or aren't, but because of all you are. To hate or be angry with you is to hate and be angry with myself, because there are not two people in the world as much alike as we are."

The waitress came back and this time we let her fill our cups. I sat there wanting to say so much and at the same time having no idea what to say.

"Jackie, listen to me now. Today is today, kiddo, and it's all that we have. Yes, we can never get that time back, but if we move forward today then we don't ever, ever have to do this again."

My own composure teetering on edge, I grabbed her hand and said, "I am here for you now, sweetie. I am here for you now."

That's when we both realized that our solution to all our stress had been to unplug completely for a while. We both chastised each other for a few minutes lightly and in a language we both clearly understood. Then we promised to learn from our mistakes and do better in the future. I guess it really does take a lifetime to grow up after all.

# CHAPTER 52

**AFTER ABOUT A** gallon of coffee and all the great self-analysis we could handle for one day, we decided what we needed was an airport fix. Riding back to the airport, we noticed that the sky was starting to clear and the clouds were starting to lift up higher. We both thought it just might clear enough for me to leave in another hour or two.

We closed all the opened panels on the plane, emptied the baggage compartment, checked the fuel and oil, did a pre-flight, then taxied out for takeoff. I looked up in the wing mirror to see her smiling and we laughed together through the intercom. I felt great again. A warm peace that I had not felt in so long regarding this oldest daughter of mine filled my heart and made me feel so grateful.

A Navy T-34C retrofitted with a turboprop engine was just leaving the airport after doing a touch-and-go landing.

She asked, "Hey Dad, isn't that the same type of plane you flew when you were in the Air Force?"

"It sure is. That's a T-34 and I've got about one hundred hours or so in one, but not with that particular engine. They're excellent trainers. The Navy still uses them."

I gave her a little history about the T-34s. Then I shared a short war story with her about how we used to play hide and seek games with them through the valleys of the Black Hills.

"After we finished with our little cat and mouse routine we would join back up and do slow rolls over Mount Rushmore. On our way back to the air base, one plane would slowly roll over and take pictures through the canopy while the other T-34 flew alongside." Then I added, "It was a real hoot."

She just shook her head, rolled her eyes at my need to always tell a story and laughed. We both agreed that the restoration of these fine birds at the facility in Tuscola, Illinois, was a great thing.

On takeoff I let the plane build up speed close to the runway before pulling back sharply on the stick. I climbed out on a forty-five degree angle with the smoker on and leveled out at two thousand feet.

On the way up, all I could hear from the front cockpit was "Alllll-right!"

Without even asking, I knew she was following my every move with her hands and feet lightly on the controls. I could feel her anxiously awaiting on me to level off and say, "Okay, kid, it's your plane."

She flew around the area for a while, and then did some steep clearing turns looking for other traffic. Then it was time for acrobatics! While doing a few slow rolls, loops, and hammerhead turns we both began to feel like a father and daughter team again. It felt good to have her back in the cockpit with me, if only for a little while.

After landing we reloaded the baggage compartment and topped off with fuel. It was time to leave again. I hated to leave so soon, but we knew that if I didn't leave now the weather might keep me socked in for another three or four days. I wanted to fly as far as Hannibal, Missouri, if possible.

Without a doubt the most significant observation made while on the ground was seeing Jackie wearing that WWII flying jacket with aviator shades. It felt like we were still back in the early 1940s. While taxiing out for takeoff, I wound the clock ten times again just to keep moving forward in time—at least in my mind.

Both of us sensing that there would be nothing but sadness in a long goodbye, I hugged her quickly and then stood back to look at her. She stood herself up straight, gave me a wink and a salute, turned around, and walked back to her car.

The smallest feeling of questions unasked and questions unanswered was still with me. But it was time to clear prop, I'm outta here!

As I was leaving, I circled over the middle of the field so Steve could take a picture. I waggled the wings and turned on the smoke as I passed overhead. I looked down for Jackie, but she was already gone. She had told me earlier that she couldn't watch me leave again. It was hard for both of us.

I flew southeast to intersect the Interstate highway I knew she was taking back to Kansas City. I just wanted to see her one last time. I needed to be sure I wasn't just dreaming that we had been together and that we had actually been able to start putting our life pieces back together again. Just when I was ready to give up and head east away from the highway, I spotted her Mustang Cobra through the low hanging clouds. It was still a little foggy so I wasn't able to fly low or beside her as I had planned. I throttled back to keep the same 80 mph pace she was setting down the interstate. The tender glow of our reunited spirits swirled throughout the cockpit like a warm Kansas sun. Then she slowly disappeared into the fog. When I could no longer see her taillights I waved goodbye. Waved goodbye to my daughter, this too independent, too stubborn, and too damn opinionated woman. She was no longer a child, this oldest daughter of mine.

# CHAPTER 53

**SOMEWHERE AROUND THE** middle of Missouri we ran into marginal weather again. I was down to five hundred feet and one-mile visibility several times, but, with one eye on the chart and one eye on highway 36, I was able to gradually navigate my way across the state. Le Beast likes the cooler moist air, so we made it to Hannibal ahead of schedule. At least we didn't have strong head winds coming across the state.

The clouds were starting to lift as I landed at Hannibal airport. I looked for Hannibal Hanna as I taxied towards the refueling area, but I didn't see her at first. But after shutting down the engine and turning all the switches, I saw her coming out of the weeds and walking towards the tail of the plane. She had probably been chasing one of those long-eared jackrabbits I saw at the side of the runway while landing.

Once again she wagged her tail, sat down at the edge of the elevator, and put one of her best, "Welcome to Hannibal Airport" faces. When I spoke to her, she sat up straighter and her ears perked up. Evidently, she must have remembered me from last week. Most people just remember the Stearman and not necessarily the pilot, but not Hanna. Hanna is a people dog. After I gave her a few pats on the head, she turned and walked back into the field, but not before giving me one brief last look over her shoulder. That was the last I saw of her.

A check on the weather showed that the system was starting to break up across Eastern Missouri and Western Illinois. It was beginning to combine with another larger low-pressure system working its way, slowly but deliberately, into the Ohio Valley from the south. I decided to wait awhile, then fly east as far as possible before it arrived.

While waiting, I put a fresh charge on the batteries and shared the St. Francis Fly-In story with the airport crew. They seemed genuinely interested in the whole trip. They had provided a charger, but first I had to remove it from an old 1950s tractor they used for cutting grass. Again, they offered to find space for the plane if I decided to stay overnight. It felt comforting to know we had a safe haven inside if needed.

A final check on the weather showed I had a reasonable chance of making it across Illinois today if I flew south towards St. Louis then headed back towards the east. I decided to give it a try. So, clear prop. The 1950's tractor told me we were on schedule, time-wise.

# CHAPTER 54

**LEAVING HANNIBAL BEHIND**, I flew down the Mississippi River for a while. Looking down at the small islands in the river, I thought of Mark Twain and his Huckleberry Finn. I wondered what he would have to say about life along the river today. I've always enjoyed his sharp wit and humor. Drifting farther on down the mighty Mississippi, I also wondered what Huck and Jim would think if they could look up today and see this red biplane flying across the sky.

I made it as far as Clarksville before I saw another black wall of thunderstorms and lightning southeast of St. Louis. I flew east hoping to circumnavigate my way back closer to Highway 36. I was beginning to think we should have stayed in Hannibal, but I knew I could go back if the weather got worse. I gradually worked my way northeast and closer to Springfield, but I wasn't able to make it quite all the way up to Highway 36.

It was getting later in the day and the daily thunderstorm activity was starting to get underway. I started to land at Taylorsville after I knew I wouldn't be able to make it to Decatur, but then I saw another small rainbow straight ahead. I flew towards it and found clearer skies behind it before having to turn southeast again.

Checking the chart, I saw that Cole County Airport was probably the best place to land at that point. Following the railroad tracks and a smaller highway to the south, I noticed the ceiling was starting to drop and the forward visibility was becoming somewhat limited by light rain. It was time to stop for the day. I was able weave my way around these smaller cells and found almost decent weather at the airport by the time we landed.

Cole County has a nice modern airport with several large hangers. I was able to get Le Beast inside for the night with room to spare. I had hoped to stop in Tuscola and give Jerry Adkinson a Stearman ride. Also, I wanted to see the T-34s again, but that was not to happen on this trip. I'd have to stop by some other time.

Before leaving the airport, I checked the weather for Tuesday. The Ohio valley wasn't supposed to clear out before the end of the week. It would be marginal VFR flying at best for the next few days.

At this point I felt that Mother Nature was trying to slow me down. Since she had provided a safe

harbor for me by providing rainbows for me to follow, and since she had played a large role in helping me get my daughter back, I planned to relax
a bit and try to stay at peace with her.

# CHAPTER 55

**WITHOUT A COURTESY** car available, I caught a ride into town with a local guy named Clarence, who was driving an old 1970s Bigmobile. I didn't ask the make or model; just noticed that it was about ten feet wide and at least fifteen feet long. Hey, it was a free ride and he didn't look like an ax murderer.

He asked, "Which motel are you staying at?"

I told him, "I don't care as long as it's cheap, clean, has a coffee pot, and is located reasonably close to the airport." I added, "And, hopefully, there's a good restaurant within walking distance."

After scratching his head and rolling his eyes around he exclaimed, "I know just the place yer lookin' for."

"Great, you're da man, Clarence," I replied.

"Yes, I am," he boasted with great pride.

With that little bit of encouragement, he gave me a rundown on all the sinful places to go and what to do while I was in town. To my dismay, I soon discovered that the more I talked, the faster he drove. I tried to talk less, but I was a captive audience so I just smiled and feigned an interest in his dissertation. I tightened my seat belt and hung on to the door strap as he proceeded to drive eighty to ninety miles per hour all the way into Mattoon, Illinois.

Finally he slowed down to sixty as we entered the city limits and asked, "What do you do for a living?"

I said I was, "Just a simple 1930s barnstorming pilot slowly flying my way back to the current time zone while en route to Maryland."

He rolled his eyes and scratched his head again, observed me with disbelief, dropped me at the nearest hotel, and then fled like he had fire lit under his ass. I guess he couldn't fully appreciate or comprehend the concept of time travel and barnstorming.

Mattoon is a nice town with clean hotels, friendly people, and good food at the local fast food eateries. The energy bar in Hannibal had worn off and it had been some time since having lunch in Cameron with Jackie. The steak burger with fries was a welcome treat at the end of a taxing day.

# CHAPTER 56

## *TUESDAY—DAY SEVEN*

**TUESDAY I WOKE** up to a windy, cloudy day, so I wasn't too sure what I'd find at the airport. I desperately needed cowboy coffee, and I was pleasantly surprised to find that the fast food eatery had great coffee and a good breakfast menu. After a meat lover's omelet and about a gallon of that good southern Illinois Colombian coffee, I sloshed back over to the hotel to check out.

The front desk called a cab and I went downstairs and waited for a ride to the airport. After waiting about half an hour for the taxi to arrive, I went back inside to the front desk to call for the cab again. I was wearing my flight suit, so I left my flying jacket draped over my bag outside while I went inside.

The very attractive young lady at the registration desk placed a second call for the cab, only to discover the driver had gone to the wrong hotel. By the time the taxi came, I had shared quite a few St. Francis and barnstorming stories with her. She seemed genuinely interested. We exchanged e-mail addresses and promised to stay in touch.

When I went back outside to meet the cab I noticed that my flying jacket was no longer draped over my bag. I thought, "Oh no! Not again!" My heart really sinks every time I think that I have lost that jacket. A wave of relief fell over me when I found that my jacket had fallen on the other side of my bag due to the easterly wind.

When I got back to the airport, the first thing I noticed was a small twin-engine jet commuter sitting in front of the terminal. Then, in the pilot's lounge, I noticed two well-dressed commuter pilots sitting at the weather computer terminals. I listened as they talked about how the front was moving up completely into the Ohio Valley and how most of the airports from Indiana east to the Appalachian were socked in IFR. However, since they were flying an IFR-equipped jet, they felt they wouldn't have any weather problems whatsoever.

I casually asked, "How far east do you think I could get flying minimum VFR?"

One of the pilots got up, turned his back to me, and said, "I wouldn't know, we don't fly VFR in jets."

I told him, "That's OK, I don't fly IFR in my Stearman."

Then, bolting from my seat and maneuvering for eye contact, I said, "Since you fly only IFR,

I guess you wouldn't be interested in buying a slightly used, older, battery-powered, handheld GPS. And, oh yeah, maybe a few used VFR charts just in case you have an electrical system failure over West Virginia?"

He walked away talking to himself and shaking his head. Having been a charter pilot for a short period of time after leaving the Air Force, I could relate to their lifestyle, but not his lofty attempt at condescension.

# CHAPTER 57

**I SAT DOWN** at one of the computers to check the weather for myself. The other pilot, Dan, tried to apologize on behalf of his comrade.

"I'm sorry. He's one of those high-time IFR pilots who thinks all air space belongs to him and should only be flown IFR."

I simply shrugged my shoulders and said, "Too bad. Maybe he'll lighten up someday and learn how to enjoy flying."

I found out that indeed the weather was continuing to deteriorate. However, I also learned there were still some minimum VFR airports along I-70 that I could get into if I needed to. So I made the decision to keep on flying as long as I could.

When Dan found out that I was flying a Stearman cross country, his face lit up and he wanted to know all about St. Francis and my trip. He also wanted to see the airplane, so I invited him over to the hanger. His enthusiasm more than made up for his partner's high and mighty attitude. He seemed genuinely interested in barnstorming, so I quickly forgot about his partner and started answering his questions.

He started by asking, "What's it like being a Barnstormer?"

I found myself explaining to him that "the basic idea behind barnstorming is to sell or give away a biplane ride to whoever wants one. You're dog tired at the end of the day, and while wiping the light film of grease from your face, you reach in your pockets, pay for your fuel and hope like hell you have made enough money for room, board, and maintenance on your old airplane. Otherwise it is sleeping bags, mosquitoes, and heavy morning dew under the wings again. The first barnstormers faced these same problems on a daily basis, but they just kept flying their old biplanes throughout the Heartland, hoping to make a few dollars by day's end."

Then he asked the same question I've had to answer at least one hundred times. "How do you become a barnstormer? I'm kinda fed up with the corporate pilot life; it's becoming more like bus driving every day."

I told him, "I know from experience how you feel, but be careful what you ask for, you might just get it. The best advice I can give you about becoming a barnstormer is DON'T! But if you do, just remember that the best way to make a small fortune in barnstorming is to start with a large fortune."

We both laughed, and then I added, "Barnstormers today come from all walks of life. They can be a doctor, lawyer, or an Indian chief. Some are retired airline pilots; others are current spray pilots, aircraft mechanics, authors, policemen, or farmers. I've known at least one of each. They're a colorful group of individuals and their common bond is biplane flying. They can be seen hanging around the fringes of an air show or antique Fly-In hustling rides between other activities."

I knew I hadn't completely answered his question when he gently interrupted and asked, "How does that compare to other types of commercial flying?"

I smiled and said, "It's a different world in a lot of ways, but like any other commercial pilot the barnstormer truly understands the limits of his environment. He respects the limits of the biplane, the weather and himself. He knows just how far to push all of them in order to survive. He has a complete knowledge of all FAA-controlled airspace rules, because these are the areas he chooses not to fly. He enjoys the freedom of less restrictive or uncontrolled VFR airspace, and that's where you will find him."

Dan scratched his chin and shook his head like he understood. He was starting to get a faraway look in his eyes—not a good sign.

# CHAPTER 58

**WHEN WE GOT** to the hanger there was another pilot there who was drooling over the Stearman. We started talking about the airplane and he asked about the types of acrobatics that a Stearman was capable of doing. He wanted to know if I'd ever done an inverted snap roll in it. I replied by saying, "No, I'm not much of an acrobatic pilot. I just like to go out and do a slow roll and maybe a hammerhead or two, an occasional loop or maybe a spin, but that's about it."

As it turned out he was an acrobatic competition pilot. He extended an invitation to see his Pitts stunt plane. It was a beauty, but that wasn't his only airplane. His other airplane was the one that I really liked, a Clipped-winged J3 Cub with a 115-hp engine on it. I thought to myself, *Sure bet Jackie would like to get her hands on that one for a hop around the patch.*

Memories of what she wrote the day after she first soloed a J3 Cub came rushing to mind as though it had been yesterday. Hard to believe that was six years ago. She was still very excited when she wrote:

*I sit here this morning already regretting the fact that I did not write my memories down last night. Last night when they were so fresh that I could still smell the honeysuckle that nearly suffocated me. The honeysuckle that lay along the sod runway whose aroma filled up the cockpit of the Piper Cub every time I touched down. On a sultry Missouri afternoon when the temperature is ninety degrees and the humidity seventy+ percent, you fly with as many windows open as possible.*

*Looking ahead I see the runway of dark green plush carpet. Directly to the north and to the east, the waters of Lake Latawana surround it. Smiling down at the people on their speedboats with a feeling of arrogance that these poor fools thought speeding through the cool waters at thirty-forty mph is the way to beat the heat. Too bad they didn't know that just a mere three thousand feet above them the temperature was a cool sixty-five degrees. Selfishly I thought I'd just as soon have it be my secret.*

*Throttle back gently to fifteen hundred rpm... fourteen hundred...thirteen hundred...now all the way back and nose her down gently. There is the horizon, now let's try to lose it ...lose it slowly...slowly.*

*At once the aroma of the honeysuckle spills in as the front wheels touch into the sea of green, touch down with a "thump" and roll briskly along the runway. I look out to the left to make sure I am clear of the trees that lay just to the side of the runway...plenty of clearance. I look out to the right, throttle forward, right rudder in and wave to my flight instructor as he gives me a faint smile and a salute to say, "Nice Job." I muse for a moment on what his thoughts might be. I ponder briefly on whether or not it is fair to take so much credit for what I am doing or whether I learned so fast because of his great instruction and not because I am a natural (not to mention being a Stearman pilot's daughter). Four hours...that is what I soloed the tail dragger in...actually a little under that, but who's counting. I expect that back before the days of control towers, back before flaps, retract gear and VOR's, four hours would have been disgraceful, especially since I already had one hundred thirty hours in airplanes with tricycle gear.*

*Climbing through four hundred feet I nose her up, kick right rudder and bring her around slowly one hundred eighty degrees to land the other way. Such a great thing is a no wind day.*

*I cut the power back completely and just coast in, adding no more than one hundred rpm to get right over the tree tops. Touching down I decide to make it a full stop and pick up my newfound friend Marv and get him out of the heat. Stick all the way back...lightly...lightly on those rudders. I think about how delicate the touch must be when rolling, yet so strong on the right rudder when the throttle goes in to take off.*

*"Hey, you going my way?" he yells above the prop blast as he makes an imaginary circle in the air telling me to swing the airplane around and then he will get in.*

*"Man can you smell that honeysuckle?" I ask as I deeply inhale the perfumed air one last time, as though I were trying to steal the air about me, adhere it inside of my soul so as to bring it out and enjoy it selfishly in silence at later times.*

*"Yeah, isn't that something."*
*"Man I could smell it every time I came by. You ready to roll?"*
*"It's your plane, lady."*

*We climb on up to one thousand feet and head west in the general area of this yellow beauty's home airport. Such a shame, I think briefly, that this airplane, this beautiful yellow flying wing, would have a home at an airport* with two hard surface runways, an FBO, and good grief...a flight planning room. What sort of flight planning do you need to fly in this baby? You look up in the sky, open your mouth to fill it with sunshine, feel whether your hair is blowing too hard, look to your flying buddy or up further to God (which my flight instructor might ponder at times that he is), and then say, "What a beautiful day for flying, so why are we still on the ground?" Yeah, that's the only kind of flight planning you need with this airplane.

At that point, I am nowhere ready to land.
"What do you say we go loop her on the way back?"
Not hesitating a bit—"Sure! Take her up a little higher and right here will be fine."
I say, "Throw the door all the way open; I want to look out and see everything."
"Sure thing," as he grabbed the door handle and lowered it down.
"Ready when you are," announces my brave friend in the front.
"Hang on! Here we go!"

Nose down...full power...one hundred...one hundred ten...one hundred fifteen...back so gently...

I see the multi-colored horizon approaching through the greenhouse window as I smile at the sounds of Marv singing some festive tune about Morocco. I pull the throttle back and howl out in my own excitement. Time froze just for those few seconds. There was absolutely nothing more important at that moment than to feel the wind and to look out past the wing at the horizon now above me...feel the slight force of gravity threatening to lift me gently out of my seat...listen to my very off-tune friend singing his happy song. It could not have been a more perfect circle if the good Lord above had drawn it Himself.

Coming to the bittersweet realization that our time has ended for the day, I turn her to the West and cut the power to come down. I reminisce on what it has taken me to get to this point. Just a few short weeks ago, aggravated after my fourth botched try at landing the Cub, I was completely without faith. Over and over again I had said to myself that I was never going to do this right, and who the heck really wanted to fly an old piece of junk tail dragger anyway...No sir, it just wasn't for me. But I knew in my soul that I had somehow been brought to this. So convincing myself of that feeling of sheer joy I would have once I had accomplished it, I kept throttling forward, lifting her tail up and climbing toward the big blue sea in the sky, coming back around to try it again. It had been almost a week before I had come back. During that time I must have visualized landing her a thousand times. Sometimes with

*Marv, shutting off his headsets and pretending to ignore me, sometimes by myself drifting forever in the lightness of the plane, and sometimes with my dad who had taught me about making your dreams of flight come true by first seeing, feeling, and tasting them in your mind. When I came around to land her this time I remembered those thousand landings and how they felt.*

*After about my third almost perfect wheel landing, Marv amusingly had asked, "So who did you go out with in the past week and practice landings with?"*
*"Nobody man, I have just seen them in my mind."*
*"Well that's good. That is the way to do it sometimes."*

*I wondered for a moment if he really knew what I had meant. It didn't really matter because I knew. I also knew at that moment that I had finally found where my connection in the sky was. So long I had wondered and experimented. Experimented with the Cessnas and their impressive instrument panels, flying from ADF to VOR and back again. Experimented with throwing myself wildly into the relative wind, feeling my body build up to terminal speed at thirty-forty seconds before I open my canopy. At last my experimenting had come to an end. At that moment, tightening my hand around the control stick, first looking at the control panel and its wonderful lack of instruments, then at my newfound friend, and then out the open window into the world below, I knew that I had finally found my home in the sky.*

Knowing that she had finally developed the "feel of being one" with her Cub, I was almost overjoyed when she shared that great experience with me later that evening. I remembered experiencing those same feelings myself, first in a Cub, then later in a Stearman. I was excited and very happy for her, and I was more proud of her that day than when she got her Private Pilot's license.

It felt good to have her back in my life again, and we were looking forward to all the great flying times that we would share in the future. Yesterday in Cameron, we had both agreed that it's a good character trait to show anger fast with righteous indignation, but an ever better trait to forgive and move on in life.

The FBO (fixed base operator) at Cole County loaned me a battery charger and I placed a quick charge on the main battery. Then we pulled the plane out to fill it with gas. While taxiing out for takeoff, I noticed Dan standing at attention next to the commuter jet and waving. We exchanged salutes as I passed by, while the other pilot busied himself with luggage from a stretch limousine. He acted like he was too involved with his IFR commuter pilot duties to acknowledge us. At this point it became obvious to me that he probably wouldn't be making me an offer on the GPS.

The encounter with the commuter pilots had taken me back to the early '70s when I had likewise been a part of their world. I wound the eight-day clock ten times again.

# CHAPTER 59

**AFTER LEAVING COLE** County Airport, it didn't take me long to realize that I would probably be in and out of minimum VFR weather again today. My game plan was to gradually work my way back North to Indianapolis and follow Interstate 70 to Richmond, Indiana, then stop there for fuel. If the weather was clear enough, maybe I could take a few skydivers for rides.

Flying into another headwind, I decided to stay under the controlled airspace around Indianapolis to conserve fuel. The ceiling was too low to go above the control area anyway. Guess I'd have to do that slow roll over the speedway next time.

Around noon I landed in Richmond with a lower ceiling and a haze in the area that limited the forward visibility to about two miles. There were no jumpers around and only one person there to handle the refueling. I shared a short version of my trip with him, grabbed a fast cup of Colombian coffee, refueled, and then headed east again. I wanted to keep flying as long as the weather would permit.

Cruising along south of I-70, I managed to circumnavigate the low-lying scud across Indiana and Ohio and remain clear of the controlled areas. I flew from airport to airport and managed to keep going and stay legal most of the time.

I would not recommend that any pilot try this type of flying, anywhere, anyway, anytime. Even in absolutely uncontrolled airspace, it's a crapshoot to fly minimum VFR.

# CHAPTER 60

**FLYING EAST AND** looking through the haze around the left side of the windshield, and then around the right side, I found myself kicking in a little rudder during this oscillation to increase my forward visibility. I had just started getting into the groove and singing a Ray Charles version of "America the Beautiful" when I suddenly realized I wasn't alone. From out of nowhere a 600 horsepower Ag Cat had slowly moved up on my right side and joined me in the swing of things. The pilot waved and smiled and then turned his smoker on to say, "Caught ya." I returned a blast of smoke and waved. Using hand signals he pointed towards the ground and invited me to follow him. So I did.

Shortly thereafter he started to descend towards a cornfield. At first I thought he was going to land, but I didn't see a runway. Then I realized he was just going to spray the corn. I stayed a couple of hundred feet above while he made his first run just to observe his technique and to check the field for wires and other obstacles. Again, he blew some smoke and wagged his wings as an invitation to join in the fun.

After descending and giving him proper distance I shoved the stick ahead, cleared the trees, and joined him on the upwind side in order to stay clear of his chemical spray drift. I knew an empty 450 hp Stearman could keep pace with a fully loaded 600 hp Ag Cat, and so did he. What he didn't know was that Le Beast had spent 25 years as a sprayer and that the current pilot had 15 seasons of spraying experience.

At the end of the field he made a downwind turn to the left to make a low spray turn, and I pulled straight up to do a slow hammerhead turn and timed it so we both entered the field at about the same time. After the ballet turns, we both knew there were experienced spray pilots over the cornfield.

At the end of the field we both pulled up over the wires with our smokers on. He made his usual downwind turn and I pulled straight up, but continued east towards Gainesville again. I tried to call him on the handheld radio on several frequencies, but there was no reply. None was needed. I made a mental note to charge the radio battery later.

# CHAPTER 61

**AFTER RUNNING IN** and out of rain I decided to take a break in Zanesville, Ohio. I thought I would probably have to stop here for the night, and I hoped I'd be able to get Le Beast inside. By the time I landed and taxied to the terminal, the rain had stopped and the sun was shining again. I parked at the terminal and took the courtesy car down the hill to get a grease burger at the local fast food eatery.

After a late lunch, a check on the weather revealed that it wasn't changing a lot. There were still several minimum VFR airports along I-70, so I decided to keep going. I knew I could always come back to the Zanesville Airport if needed. I wanted to make it as far as Washington County Airport in Pennsylvania. There I knew I could find a safe haven for both man and Beast.

Somewhere between Zanesville and Washington County Airport, the weather started to clear. I was just a few miles northwest of West Virginia. Looking down at the GPS, I shook my head and remembered the last time it crapped out on me thirty or forty miles south of here.

As the foothills began to slowly slide beneath the plane, I began thinking about heading southeast across the West Virginia Mountains again. The GPS had been accurate the few times I had checked it over the past two days. I decided to turn it on as a backup, as I gradually turned southeast with my barnstorming finger on the chart. I knew I could always find my way back to I-70 by flying straight north again. Shortly after crossing over into West Virginia at Moundsville, I began to notice rain clouds moving up from the south. Regardless of what the GPS was indicating, I doubted that I could fly direct to Morgantown without getting wet, so I headed back east towards Waynesburg, Pennsylvania.

After passing Waynesburg, I flew southeast again for a while until I saw lightning on the mountain peaks and in the valley ahead. Had I followed the GPS I would have been closer to the lighting and in the valley at that point. While staring at another black wall of thunderstorms, I looked for another rainbow of safety to pass through, but there was none to be had. So I decided to turn around and land at the Waynesburg Airport.

A rain shower had already moved through the airport area earlier, and several pockets of water remained on the runway. On landing, the tail wheel tried to come up every time I ran through a pocket of water, and then we hydroplaned across it until we hit pavement again. It was not the best landing of the trip and I probably washed half of the grease out of the wheel bearings.

# CHAPTER 62

**TAXIING UP TO** the terminal with wet and grabbing brakes, I looked down at the wet wings and ask Le Beast, "Are we having fun yet?" There was no reply, but I could almost feel Mother Nature grinning at me again.

Waynesburg has only a few small hangers and one or two larger hanger/workshop buildings. I wasn't surprised when the attendant at the counter told me there wasn't any available space inside. Then a fellow spoke up and volunteered to let us stay in one of the workshops. He had to leave a Cessna 170 outside to accommodate us, but he assured me that it was not a problem. We both knew a metal Cessna could weather outside overnight better than a Stearman. And then he gave me a ride into town. Talk about hospitality.

The televised weather that evening showed an occluded (stalled) front stretching the full length of the western side of the Appalachian Mountains.

The forecast indicated that this front wouldn't be moving for a few more days, since another system moving up the coast on the eastern side was keeping it stationary.

The thought of spending a few days in Waynesburg wasn't unpleasant at all. It was a nice area with friendly people and the plane was high, dry, and safe. But I wanted to get home after a week on the road, and I needed to get ready for the banner flying and biplane rides by the weekend. I knew if I could get over the hills, I'd be trying to make it home tomorrow. Also, I knew if I'd been flying a commuter jet, I'd be home by now. But I wouldn't be having nearly as much fun.

Later I called home to update the girls on my whereabouts and the adventures of the day. I told them how much I missed them and that I hoped to be home in a day or so.

A short time later the phone rang. This time it was Jackie. She got my phone number from the girls and was calling to check on me. I had been thinking about her earlier while flying through the canyons. Her voice on the phone was still a little hesitant, but it felt so good to have her back in my life again. I thought about times in the past few years when I didn't want to admit to myself that there was something missing with her not being there. It was a void that I both ignored and refused to let myself consider. There were times I sat out back of the house thinking of her while watching the sun go down across the water, and I felt a lump rising from my chest to my throat. My reaction to this was to get up and stop watching the sunset. I refused to let my mind go there.

I was sure that there were some hurdles for her and me to go over later, but I truly felt in my heart that we could work things out together. There was still regret when I thought of things lost, but it was overshadowed by the hope of what the future held for us. So much pain and anger seemed to have lifted and simply floated up and away into the sky above me. And, at last, I felt like I was finally beginning to understand the plans John Grace had for me in the dream.

# PART V

## - AGAINST ALL ODDS -

# CHAPTER 63

## *WEDNESDAY—DAY EIGHT*

**EARLY WEDNESDAY MORNING** I called flight service for a weather update, after a cup of delicious left-over motel coffee. The fronts were still entrenched on both sides of the Appalachians, and all airports on the eastern side were reporting IFR conditions as far south as Richmond, Virginia. Some improvement was forecast for the afternoon, but only a few airports close to the mountains would have VFR conditions.

Flying VFR today meant that I would have to stay close to foothills and fly south the full length of West Virginia, then cross over into central Virginia. Once into Virginia, my plan was to fly south of Richmond to the coastline, then up the Delmarva Peninsula to Cambridge Airport in Maryland. It would be a longer trip, but I felt that I could make it home by the end of the day—if Mother Nature was kind to me.

Over ham and eggs and several cups of good airport coffee, I offered to buy a late breakfast for the maintenance shop owner, but he declined. He also declined payment for the night's lodging for Le Beast. I think he just liked old planes and was pleased to have us as his guests. I thanked him for his hospitality and did a final weather check before heading south for West Virginia.

Walking from the restaurant back to the shop, I had noticed a 1977 Harley Davidson motorcycle parked outside a hanger. It must be the same everywhere: pilots love their old cars, old motorcycles, and old airplanes. For years I've had a 1976 Honda 400CL Super Sport in the back of the hanger. We pulled the plane from the hanger, refueled, and then it was clear prop time again. I wound the eight-day clock ten turns and made a mental note of June 1977.

# CHAPTER 64

**THE MID-MORNING** air was cool with light wind and no rain as I followed Interstate 79 to Morgantown. The weather east towards the mountains appeared clear as we passed by Interstate 68 leading to Cumberland, Maryland. Even if I could have made it over the hills, I knew it was IFR at the Cumberland Airport.

We headed south down the full length of the wild and wonderful state of West Virginia. There was a lot of rugged terrain to cross, but it was beautiful low-mountain country with several crystal clear lakes and I enjoyed the long ride.

After singing "Country Roads" a few dozen times, I finally landed at Raleigh County Airport in the southern part of the state. I even had enough spare time to make up a few dirty versions of the song along the way.

It was past lunchtime, so I decided to take a break, stretch my legs, and get a snack after

refueling. There was no sassy waitress or club sandwich to be had on this day, but I did manage to
get a snack and some iced tea from a vending
machine.

Another check on the weather before takeoff
showed that the system in the east was still stagnant north of central Virginia. My planned route
would keep me just south of this area. And then it
was time to clear prop again.

# CHAPTER 65

**FLYING OUT ALONG** Interstate 64 and heading east again, I was able to see the Allegheny Mountain range off in the distance. If the weather forecast held true, it would remain clear over the Appalachian and Shenandoah Valley areas for most of the afternoon. I had my doubts.

The Interstate through that part of West Virginia and Virginia snakes through the mountain valleys like spaghetti. With a ceiling that kept me from flying over the tops of the mountains, I had no choice but to follow the highway. Winding around through the valleys, with mountains on both sides, I began to slowly sing a very serious version of, "Country Roads"—take me home, please!

After crossing over White Sulphur Springs, the terrain gradually began to run downhill towards the Shenandoah Valley of Virginia. It was hazy in the valley, and the slick highway below spoke of recent rain in the area. There were two more small valleys that I would have to pass through before getting into the more wide-open valley floor.

Everything was going well until I was halfway across the first valley. At that point, I suddenly realized that a weirdly diffused green cloud had slowly drifted in behind us. An eerie lead-blue sky was looming over the mountain peaks, and in all directions we were being surrounded by a greenish-blue mist rising from the valleys and gullies below, like marsh gas from a swamp.

It wasn't scary and I wasn't frightened at first, but then I suddenly felt fragile and threatened by this unexpected turn of events. I rationalized that it was some type of industrial smoke, but I didn't see any obvious source within my limited visual range. The farther I flew into the valley, the thicker the fog became.

A quick check of the chart showed there were two private airstrips south of the interstate. Due to the haze and smoke, I was unable to find either one when I circled south of the highway. I descended a couple hundred feet and made several turns while looking down through swampy mist for a safe haven below. Then I looked up only to discover that the open canyon to the east had suddenly disappeared into a dense fog rising from it.

As I made a slow one-hundred-eighty-degree climbing turn, I could feel the hair on the back of my neck starting to rise. With a mild case of claustrophobia starting to surface, I decided to head back towards the west and get the hell out of there.

Then I saw another large keyhole clearing to the east. I flew towards the opening, kept going, and was able to eventually pass through the valley. Looking over my shoulder as we cleared the canyon walls, I shook my head and said aloud, "Man, was that ever weird."

# CHAPTER 66

**THE SECOND SMALL** valley we had to fly through had a three-thousand-foot mountain on each side. The highway ran straight for about ten miles, and then it doglegged to the right for another mile or so before opening into the flatland.

I couldn't see over the top of either side of the valley, but I thought I had enough room to turn around at the lower end if the opening wasn't clear. It felt like I was flying into a blind alley.

Then, just before reaching the end of the valley where I would have to turn right or turn around, I ran into rain. It had dumped over the mountain from the southeast and was threatening to close the mouth of the valley.

My first thought was to make a sharp, climbing, one-hundred-eighty-degree reverse turn to the left (known as a chandelle) and head back west. I was beginning to feel trapped and that seat cushion thing was happening again. But I suddenly remembered the first valley behind me and I had serious doubts about being able to fly back through that eerie fog. As I descended beneath the rain, I decided to keep going to have a look at the dogleg exit from the valley.

I could see light through the canyon below the rain, so I added full power, lowered the nose, and made a run for it. About halfway through the canyon I was in heavy rain and just a few feet above the trees, but I could still see the highway and the clear valley ahead.

With a solemn resolve, I kept lowering the nose and building up speed to punch my way through to the valley below. I usually cruise between 100 and 110 mph. The airspeed indicator was registering 175 to 180, and the flying wires were starting to sing at a constant high pitch, and then I broke through the rain and entered that beautiful, sun-drenched, open area of the Shenandoah Valley.

It felt good to be back in an open area with sunshine and broken clouds overhead. A quick look back into the closed canyon caused me to shake my head, again. I thought to myself, *Damn Appalachians just had to try to kick my ass one more time.*

I was glad there wasn't any hail in the storm, and I was relieved to be out of the mountains. I had only one smaller canyon to pass through and then I would finally be clear of the valley and back on the coastal flatlands.

# CHAPTER 67

**FOR AWHILE THE** sun was warm and the wind was calm as I flew north along the Interstate up through the Shenandoah Valley. It was the first time I had felt the warm sun since leaving Kansas on Sunday.

While drifting along at two hundred feet, a faint smell of honeysuckle and fresh-cut hay gently wafted up from the valley floor. The picturesque towns along the river and the small farms manicuring the gentle rolling hills make this lush green valley one of the most beautiful areas on the entire East Coast. It's no small wonder that Denise and I had decided to spend our honeymoon here about twenty-five years ago.

By the time I turned back east at Staunton and headed towards Charlottesville, it was starting to get hazy again. After passing Waynesboro the forward visibility dropped to about two miles and there was no definite ceiling.

The mouth of the canyon looked clear at first, but when I turned northeast to fly through the pass I could see a lightning-filled rainstorm blocking the entire valley. A few late-day storm cells had already topped the three-thousand-foot Mountains north of the highway, and I started to notice a few rain-drops on the windshield. I knew passage through this area was impossible, so I started an immedi-ate one-hundred-eighty-degree turn to the right.

About forty-five degrees into the turn, a blast of air rushing from the mouth of the canyon lifted both left wings to the vertical position, and the engine revved up to redline rpm when the prop hit the dead air space created by the blast. I stomped on the left rudder pedal and shoved the stick forward and to the left, hoping to stop the roll and get back into solid air again.

After hanging in that position and losing alti-tude and airspeed for what seemed an eternity, the plane finally leveled, but I was headed straight towards a three-thousand-foot mountain. A slow, climbing, chandelle turn to the right was my best option.

I said to myself, "Russ, you bonehead, I don't think you have enough time or altitude to do a chandelle," but I knew it was my only option.

Slamming the stick forward and hoping to build up the speed I needed for the turn, the airspeed slowly started to increase from an almost stalled 50 mph. It seemed like forever before the airspeed picked up to 60, then 70, and 80...I knew I would need at least 120 mph before starting a turn that would climb us to safety.

The altimeter was winding down too fast; we were at 2500 feet and headed down to 2300, 2100...I estimated that we could go no lower than 1500 feet minimum before having to make a turn or crash. I felt like a suicidal kamikaze pilot heading towards the base of the mountain. Gaining speed too slow at 90 mph, 95, 100, and losing altitude too fast at 2000 feet, 1800...My hands were starting to sweat, my breathing rate increased, and I could hear my heart beating in my ears. Then at 1600 feet and 120 mph I started a shallow right turn and pulled back on the stick and started a steep, climbing turn up the side of the mountain.

The G force from the climb shoved me down into the seat hard as I watched the trees grow larger beneath the wings. I wanted to pull back harder on the stick, but knew if I did the plane would do a high-speed stall to the left and slam me into the mountain. While holding the same pressure on the stick, I felt a sudden vibration and heard a whomp-thump-whomp sound as I watched the top of a tall pine tree slide past the right wing tip. I knew that I had just flown the landing gear through the top of a tree. I waited for the crash...and waited...and waited...

Then, after another thump and another tree-top, I slowly began to pull away from the trees and fly away from the canyon wall. As we leveled off below the rain and headed towards Waynesboro, I slowly began to breathe again.

The grim reaper would have to wait for another day. After I quit shaking and my heartbeat slowed down, I thought of how I'd placed this fifty-year-old biplane and myself in a position that could easily have destroyed us a dozen times, or at minimum caused both of us harm beyond recognition. So many times I have chased this dream known as barnstorming. Why have I chosen this dream instead of just staying home and flying for a living or being happy and content with restoring antique aircraft?

I checked the chart and found that there were two airports in the area. Eagles Nest Airport was about two miles northwest of Waynesboro, and Shenandoah Valley Airport was about fifteen miles north. With this fast-moving storm working its way to the north, Eagles Nest was the best choice for a quick landing. The rain I ran into in the canyon was now dumping over the entire west face of the mountain just east of the city.

Flying west again, I searched the area hoping to find Eagles Nest Airport. I had looked for it earlier as I was heading east, but a storm cell and low visibility had prevented me from seeing it. The storm cell was still lingering north of the highway, so I passed by the area a second time, again without seeing it.

Instinctively, I entered a holding pattern south of the highway to weigh my options. It was a survival habit: mentally removing myself from the situation, like an out-of-body experience. It was time for an outsider look at what was happening. I knew

I couldn't fly north to Shenandoah Airport, and I couldn't fly east through the canyon. There were no airports west, and I wasn't sure I had enough gas to fly south to another private strip on the map that I was unable to find earlier. I knew I had to find Eagles Nest.

Flying a wider circle north of the highway in search of the ever-elusive airport, we ran into rain—again. Just when I was ready to head south and take my chances on finding the private strip, I looked down at the GPS and decided to give it one final chance to redeem itself. With a skeptical glance, I said, "Whatever you do, don't give me a wrong reading now, sucker." I turned it on while circling and it soon found its coordinates. I punched in W13 for Eagles Nest, and waited.

Eventually it locked in and gave me an indication that the airport was five miles northeast of my present position. I thought, *OK baby, don't fail me now.* I lowered the nose, descended a couple hundred feet for better visibility, and then headed into the rain. In about two minutes I looked around the side of the wet blurry windshield, and there, on the nose, was Eagles Nest Airport. And a wall of rain was rapidly moving down the hills from the east headed directly towards the airport.

I knew there would be a lot of gusty wind ahead of the storm, so I made a fast pass over the field to check the windsock before landing. The windsock was extended straight out and favoring a landing to the northeast, but barely. I circled to the left and came around to set up for another tricky one-wheel landing like the one I had successfully made last week at Norton, Kansas.

Heading straight towards the runway with the right wing cocked down into the wind, I looked down at the windsock again. At first glance it appeared that the wind was straight across the runway, but my ground speed didn't feel right. We were going too fast. As I crossed the threshold of the runway, a quick glance towards the windsock showed the wind had shifted towards the south. I now had a quartering tailwind. A quartering tail-wind, for an airplane with a reputation for ground looping, is bad news. And at that ground speed I knew I would use a third of the runway before even getting one wheel on the ground. A quick look towards the east at the imminent storm con-vinced me there would not be time to take off and reverse directions to land into the wind. Since I didn't have enough fuel to fly elsewhere, I had no choice but to land straight ahead.

Reducing the power from 1100 rpm to 900...800...I held my breath and waited for the right wheel to touch down. When it finally made contact I gradually dropped the rpm back to 700. Then, at the halfway point of a fast-disappearing runway, the plane slowed down enough to plant the left gear on the pavement. A sudden gust of quartering tailwind tried to shove the plane side-ways, as I struggled with the rudder and brakes to stay straight on the runway. I immediately reduced all power and pulled the tail wheel com-pletely down while slowly applying first left brake then right brake to stay straight on the final fourth of the runway. As I began to slow down, the wind made one final attempt to lift the tail back up. I brought it back down with a quick blast of power and prop wash. And then I applied full brakes and waited, as the white fence gate at the end of the runway disappeared from sight beneath the engine cowling. The plane finally stopped about fifty yards from the end of the runway. At that point, I knew I would have to buy a new seat cushion when I got home.

I immediately parked over a tie-down space facing east, shut the engine down, turned the master switch off, then jumped from the cockpit and tied the plane down just before the wind and rain hit. I grabbed my hat and cockpit cover from the baggage compartment, strapped the controls into place with the seat belt, hooked the cockpit cover bungee cords into place, then headed for shelter.

Safely inside, I looked through the terminal window and watched from a distance of two hundred feet as Le Beast slowly disappeared inside a torrential rain-driven thunderstorm. I watched helplessly as the titanic wind tried to lift the plane off the ground and rip it loose from the tie-down ropes. Water was gushing from the bottom of the engine cowling like an overflowing down spout. The wings rocked back and forth and the tail surged upwards against its restraint. Waves of driving rain rolled across the wings and fell at the trailing edge like an angry waterfall. Mother Nature was extremely pissed at me for flying today, and she was giving new meaning to the saying, "Hell hath no fury like a woman scorned."

The lady behind the counter inside the terminal hadn't noticed the wind shift earlier, but she did comment on how fast I seemed to be taxiing towards the end of the runway. I didn't bother to tell her I was still landing. Instead I said, "Oh yeah, I just wanted to get it tied down before the rain hit."

# CHAPTER 68

**AFTER ABOUT FORTY-FIVE** minutes, the rain stopped and the wind settled down a bit, so I went back outside to check the plane. The corner of the right rear cockpit cover had folded itself inside the cockpit, and a bowl of water was sitting on the rear seat. I lifted it clear of the seat and let it slowly drain inside the fuselage and exit past the tail wheel. As it drained past the seat, I was very careful about not getting my new friend, the GPS, wet. It had really saved my bacon that day and I decided, then and there, to start trusting it again.

A loose bungee cord from the cockpit cover had punched a hole in the fabric beneath the baggage compartment. I planned to do a temporary repair with the duct tape I had in the tool kit. Every good barnstormer carries a roll of duct tape and lacing wire.

I opened a few panels hoping to dry things out while it wasn't raining. As I walked to the front of the plane, I discovered that the leading edges of both upper and lower wings were bare of paint in several areas. Evidently, when I blasted my way through that second canyon, there had been some light hail embedded inside the rainstorm. I knew I would have to do some painting when I got back to Maryland.

It was completely drenched and water was still dripping down from the engine cowling and off the trailing edges of the wings. The last of the wax I had applied in Kansas was definitely gone. There was a small piece of pine tree limb still hanging in the left landing gear fork, but otherwise everything appeared to be in pretty good shape. The Stearman is a tough machine.

While looking down the runway towards the south, I replayed the landing in my mind. I realized how damn lucky I was to get the plane on the ground with that quartering tail wind. Landing five minutes later would have been a catastrophe, even if I could have landed into the wind. In the last few seconds of the landing I had almost decided to lock one brake and let the plane ground loop to a painful stop. I thought that would have been a better alternative than flipping it on its back after hitting the split rail fence. If it had not stopped, that's exactly what I had planned to do. All the time and money I had spent on maintaining the brakes had finally paid off.

# CHAPTER 69

**KNOWING I WOULD** definitely not be flying any-more that day, I went in search of dry hanger space for the plane overnight. The only space available was in another maintenance hangar, but the door opening wasn't high enough for the upper wing to get all the way inside. Poor Le Beast would have to weather out the rain and wind again tonight.

At first I didn't feel comfortable leaving the plane outside at a small and unsecured airport, but a very friendly and helpful airline pilot living next to the airport had assured me that it would be safe overnight. I closed the open panels, replaced the cockpit cover, installed the engine cover, checked the tie-down ropes, grabbed my flight bag, and caught a cab to Waynesboro.

By the time I got into Waynesboro it had started to rain again. The taxi driver gave me the local weather report, which stated that the rain would continue all night and most of tomorrow. At that point I couldn't even think about tomorrow. I was just glad to have my barnstorming ass safely on the ground again, especially after the beating it had taken today. And I was extremely glad that the arrogant commuter pilot at Cole County Airport had not taken me up on the offer to buy the GPS.

I checked my wet, tired, and hungry body into a local motel and collapsed on the bed for a while. After a shower and fresh dry clothes, I ate a large steak with all the trimmings at the nearest restaurant. It was some of the best food I'd had on the trip, but it wasn't nearly as delicious as St. Francis barbecued beef on a bun. After eight days on the road, I was looking forward to the fresh seafood I knew we would have at home on the weekend—if I were home by then.

I called home to report that I'd run into a little weather over the hills and would have to hold up until it cleared. They were a little disappointed, but otherwise understood. I promised to be home for the weekend, for sure. They said Jackie had called and was concerned about the weather for the next few days and that I should call her. I promised I would.

A final check on the weather, before retiring for the day, indicated that another slow moving coastal system was pushing north out of the Carolinas behind the already stagnant weather lying just north of Richmond. It appeared that we were starting into an early "dog days of summer" period, and I could find myself socked in for several days before it cleared.

# CHAPTER 70

## *BARNSTORMING*

**LATER THAT EVENING** I began to reflect on several events of the past and some nagging thoughts about this illness known as barnstorming began to emerge—again. Why was I doing this? What kind of a masochist was I anyway? All that money and all that time I spent—for what? Am I insane? I'd be a millionaire today if only I had kept my head out of the clouds and stayed away from those damned old biplanes. But, no, here I am—again—living the life of a gypsy, just so I can fly.

Why are we barnstormers so fixated, cursed, and possessed with this idea? Almost all of the true barnstormer's conscious moments are absorbed in how to spend more time in the air with his mistress. This is the one adulteress his spouse will forgive, because she knows he is truly a sick man. When he's not flying, most of his time is spent at the airport pampering and talking to his "lady friend." He would probably lie, cheat, and steal just to have his way with her for a few moments together in the sky. He's worse than a junkie when it comes to flying old biplanes. Would he give up this sickness and addiction? Probably, but not by choice, and definitely not in this lifetime.

Barnstormers fly in the past, but somehow manage to live in the present, without concern for the future. He's not the aviator that will spend half the day planning and charting his course through a control area just to impress you with his skills and latest navigation and communication gadgets. Nor will he spend nights awake worrying about the next day's weather.

He is the type of flier who will knock on your door and drag your ass out of bed at four a.m. to go flying in whatever weather Mother Nature has blessed the earth with on that day. He will shove a cup of coffee in your hand, and then drive out in the boonies to an old hanger at an uncontrolled airport. The only noise to be heard at this time of day is a meadowlark or the distant yapping of a fox or coyote.

The silence of the morning is interrupted first by the sound of the hanger doors opening, and then by the roar of an old radial engine as it barks to life. Climbing into the front cockpit of a fifty-year-old biplane devoid of instruments, then breathing in the sweet smoke from the warming radial engine before dawn, is a brain-jolting experience. (Who needs drugs?)

Then, while watching the sun as it slowly rises up from the ocean along the coast, or over a cornfield in the Heartland, the experience of the earth coming alive across America for another day gives one an overwhelming feeling of being born again. At the end of the day, this same flier will land you into a bright orange sunset over the Rocky Mountains, or high above the Georgia Plains, and let you experience the true beauty of flying at dusk.

Between dawn and dusk he just might feel obligated to turn your ass upside down and inside out in the old biplane, and show you what life looks like a few hundred feet above the trees. Along the way he'll point out hawks, eagles, and other fliers that share this freedom known as flight. Other unseen points of interest not seen from the ground might include a family of foxes at the end of an overhanging bluff, or a pile of 1930s automobiles and farming machinery, dumped along a gulch at the back of a farm in Nebraska to prevent soil erosion.

While flying a few feet off the ground and waving to the Ohio farmers with a flock of sea gulls behind their plows, or while doing a slow roll over Chesapeake Bay fishermen as they slowly drift along harvesting their catch for the day, the flier waggles the wings. Each wave to the other in recognition of their coexistence. No words are spoken; none are needed.

This flier will not show you the big cities or the congested highways that the aviator will point out with pride, as he talks to the air traffic controllers who steer him and his aircraft along the airways. These are the areas that a flier avoids like the plague. His purpose is to observe and show the beauty of the land, and the beauty of the American people as they begin and end their days. By day's end he will not have left a footprint in the sky or anywhere on the land, but he will have created memories and brought pleasure to those few that have shared his presence.

At the end of this experience, you will climb down from the cockpit with the smell of burnt oil swirling about, and there will probably be a few spots of oil on your goggles. Your life will never be the same again. There will be a special glow in your heart and an awakening to your spirit never experienced before that day. Long after you have forgotten the pilot's name, you will still remember the biplane ride. This flier is a daydreamer and a wind chaser, and he will leave you with memories that will last a lifetime. It is that love of flying and the sharing of that experience that keeps him going. That's who a barnstormer is and that's what flying with him is all about.

I drifted off to sleep later, knowing there was nothing else in this world that I would rather be doing. I was a happy and contented barnstormer, and that was enough.

# PART VI

## - THE FINAL DAY -

# CHAPTER 71

## *THURSDAY—DAY NINE*

**WAKING UP THURSDAY** morning to the sound of rain beating on the motel window, I gave serious thought to turning over and going back to sleep. Then I decided to get up and see what was shaking for the day. After having some thick motel coffee, I *watched AM Weather,* only to confirm that the system was still somewhat stagnant without favorable conditions for change for a few days.

After a leisurely breakfast of Virginia ham and eggs, I drank about a half-gallon of decent coffee with chicory. It wasn't Colombian coffee, but it was a far cry better than motel mud coffee. I had a nice little caffeine buzz going, so I was ready to go again. I headed for the airport to check on Le Beast.

Pools of water were lying in all the low places around the airport. I could tell by the sag in the cockpit and engine covers that the plane was completely saturated. The fabric under the fuse-lage had begun to sag in several places. It was really a wet duck. It had stopped raining and there was a light breeze, so I began opening all fuselage and wing panels and removing covers to dry it out. I knew from experience that it would take half a day before the fabric would dry and shrink back into place.

I decided to start the engine and let it warm up and taxi up and down the runway to blow some of the internal moisture away. I wanted to be ready if the weather happened to clear enough to fly later in the day. I drained copious amounts of fuel from the wing and engine petcocks to be sure there weren't any water in the system. After adding two quarts of oil and priming the fuel system, I climbed into the cockpit, yelled "Clear Prop!", and hit the starter button. The engine turned over a few times, but it wouldn't start. Thinking I had probably not primed it enough, I pumped the throttle a few times and tried again. It churned and churned, but it would not fire. After a third attempt at prim-ing and churning, I knew it was not going to start. Then the battery finally ran down and the starter ground to a stop.

Dudley, the helpful airline pilot, came to my rescue again. I needed a battery charger and a long extension cord to reach the plane. I removed part of the engine cowling and found a pool of water on top of the engine case. The inside of the compartment looked like it had been sprayed down with a garden hose. I wiped the area as dry as possible and left it to dry as the battery was charging.

While the plane was drying and the battery was charging, I walked around and looked at the other aircraft in the large hanger. There were a few tail wheel planes inside and a glider or two in the back part of the hanger. It was my kind of airport.

With a fresh charge on the battery, I hit the starter button and watched as the prop turned over and over. As it turned I nursed the throttle ahead and said, "Come on now, sweetheart. Come on, darling. Start, you asshole!" Finally, I was almost starting the engine, but it was missing, backfiring, and barely running on one magneto. When I tried to switch it to the left mag, it would shut down completely. I knew the left magneto was either dead or, more likely, saturated with water.

After removing the one-foot access panels from around the engine, I was finally able to remove the cover plate from the back of the left magneto. Access to the backs of the mags is limited to barely two inches from the front of a stainless steel firewall. The inside of the cover was damp so I knew I definitely had a wet mag problem. Using a small handheld swivel mirror, I could see the points and the inside of the mag were sweating moisture also.

Memories came rushing back of a similar rainstorm in St. Francis that had drowned this engine and got one of the magnetos wet. Even with John Graces' help it had still taken me most of the day to remove the magneto, disassemble it, dry it completely out, and then reinstall it. I was hoping that I would not have to go through that same routine again. With the modified cowling I had added since then, I knew that before removing the magneto it would take half a day just to remove enough engine cowling, and probably another full day to put it back in place.

I tried to dry it out by hand with a dry cloth, and by spraying into the back of the mag with an electrical moisture spray bomb that I bought in town, but the engine was still missing and backfiring when it started. At that point I knew I would have to find some other way to dry the inside of the mag, or I would have to remove it and then dry it out. There wasn't enough room to apply heat directly from a hair dryer or heat gun, so I bent a small piece of metal to deflect some warm air into the back of the magneto. This arrangement seemed to be working quite well, until the metal got too hot to handle. Then, after burning the hair off the back of several knuckles with the heat gun, I decided to take a lunch break and contemplate the situation.

Walking back to the terminal and shaking my head I mumbled to myself, "Hey, nobody said this barnstorming game would be easy."

# CHAPTER 72

**LUNCH CONSISTED OF** one energy bar, one pack of cheese crackers, and a Dr. Pepper. (Pilot food.) After this delicious meal, I watched the weather channel on the airport TV. The weather in the valley was expected to gradually clear in the afternoon, giving us a break and maybe some sunshine. I wondered if the weather east of the hills was starting to move north or break up also. I started to call flight services for an update, but since I didn't have a flyable airplane, it really didn't matter one way or the other at that point.

After getting caught up on all the local airport gossip, I shared my trip with everyone and told them all about St. Francis. They seemed to enjoy hearing about most of the activity. I asked them if they would like to hear a few new verses of "Country Roads." Since we were in mixed company, they declined the offer, and I went back outside to work on the plane again.

Soon after charging the battery and deflecting more hot air into the back of the magneto several times, it finally started again and was running a little better. I knew I was on the right track, so I continued with that routine for another hour or so until it dried out enough to run on the left mag only without backfiring. Then, when it was dropping only 200 rpm, I was convinced that it would continue to dry out with its own internal heat while running.

# CHAPTER 73

**LOOKING UP AT** the blue sky through broken clouds, I knew that the valley was clearing as forecasted. A Cessna 182 had just landed and the pilot gave us a report.

"The weather east of the hills was starting to lift and Charlotte Airport was at minimum VFR about thirty minutes ago."

I rushed inside to call flight services for an update. They confirmed that the upper system was indeed clearing across Virginia and slowly moving north away from Richmond, but another similar system was moving its way north and would be in the area later in the day. They told me I had about a three-hour VFR window to pass through the area on my way to the coast—if I left Eagles Nest *right now*. The weather was already clear and above VFR for landing at Cambridge Airport and should stay that way all day.

I replaced and closed all opened panels, packed everything back in the baggage compartment, filled the gas tanks, and then it was "Clear Prop, I'm outta here." I thanked all the good folks for their help and promised to come back in the fall for their Fly-In, if possible. I wound the clock twelve times to make up for what seemed like ten years on the ground, and then declared the date to be June 1985. I felt like I had aged at least that much yesterday flying through the canyons.

Climbing out of Eagles Nest, I flew up through some scattered clouds at forty-five hundred feet, and looked down at the canyon and the mountain I had turned away from yesterday. A cold chill ran up my spine and the hair on the back of my neck started to raise a little as I flew over that valley and cleared the last hurdle before the flatlands. As soon as I cleared the hills, I saw a flat layer of clouds stretching as far into the distant east as I could see. Knowing I could descend through the scattered clouds anytime, I stayed above them and turned on my trusty GPS. I tuned in Charlottesville Airport and, for the first time since starting the trip, I had a slight tail wind. Cruising past Charlottesville at fifty-five hundred feet, I saw the airport through the scattered clouds.

# CHAPTER 74

**THE AIR WAS** smooth and the sun was warm on my face, and my mood really lightened when I checked the GPS and found that I was doing a whopping 150 mph groundspeed. I couldn't believe it at first, so I tuned into Orange County Airport and verified that, yes, I had at least 50 mph tailwinds. Then I switched the GPS to Shannon Airport south of Fredericksburg to again verify speed and distance. The GPS was working great, and with that much tailwind I intended to stay above the broken clouds as long as possible.

After a few minutes, I noticed that the speed and distance were staying the same, so I hit the refresh button. That's when I discovered that the son of a bitch had locked up on me again, cold turkey. At first I started to get upset, but this time I was better prepared. I gently turned on my freshly-charged handheld nav-com, tuned into Brooke VOR, and found that I was still right on course for

Shannon Airport. I definitely had no intention of hanging my neck out on one radio again—least of all that damn GPS.

At that point I had been busy with the radios and not really paying too much attention to the clouds below, which had gradually pushed us up to seventy-five hundred feet. When I started searching for Fredericksburg through the broken clouds, I soon found that I was slowly flying above an almost completely overcast area. Then, after passing Brooke VOR station, I was unable to see any ground whatsoever. A layer of light blue-gray clouds were forming overhead, and the sun slowly faded into a dusty orange ball, as we became wedged between two layers of clouds stretching northeast as far as I could see. It was déjà vu all over again.

I did an immediate one-hundred-eighty-degree turn and headed back towards Orange County Airport in order to get below the clouds. By the time I passed Fredericksburg again, the area was likewise overcast. A quick check of the chart showed I was almost at the halfway point between Eagles Nest and Cambridge Airport.

I was concerned, but not frightened. Once again, I went into a holding pattern about five hundred feet above the overcast clouds and weighed my options. I felt guilty for placing us in such peril; our souls were naked and at the mercy of Mother Nature—again. A distant ray of dark blue sky between the cloud layers in the east beckoned us to go where only ghosts of men dwell.

Backing myself slowly into the corner of the seat, I closed my eyes and forced myself to relax, breathe slowly, and then evaluate the situation like an outside observer. Unless it means life or death, it is sometimes best to pause before reacting. Somehow all the pieces of the puzzle seem to fall in place.

With 50 mph tail winds, I knew I had more than enough fuel to make it all the way to Cambridge, and I was reasonably sure I could make it back to Eagles Nest. That is, if the weather was still clear in the Shenandoah Valley. I knew the weather was clear at Cambridge, and I felt sure I could navigate clear of the restricted and controlled areas along the route with one radio. I tuned into two other VOR radio stations just to verify that the nav-com radio was still working okay. It was, so I decided to stay clear of the clouds, if possible, and head for the Chesapeake Bay.

# CHAPTER 75

**WITH THE HAND-HELD** radio plugged into a freshly-charged battery for a little extra power boost, I started gradually navigating around and between the restricted areas south of the Washington, DC, area. Then I thought to myself, *Russ, you dummy, what are you going to do if your radio fails and a Blackhawk helicopter comes up through the clouds with a 'shoot now and ask questions later' attitude? It would serve you right for trying such a dumb trick.* So far, no F-16 fighters had been scrambled out of Andrews Air Force Base to shoot us down, so we continued to "Stay with the plan" and stumble our way along.

After flying along for a while I noticed that there was no definite reference visible on the horizon. There was only an oval, milky passageway with a flat valley of fog and a ceiling of dark, cream over-cast that were slowly melding together. A sinking pit in my stomach told me it was only a matter of

time until we were completely enclosed by a fun-
neled womb of clouds.

Without instruments for descending through
what I knew would be hundreds, maybe thousands, of feet before breaking through the bottom layer, I decided to make a one-hundred-
eighty-degree turn and get the hell out of there. I
started a left turn, but soon realized that I was too
far into the funnel to make the turn. So I straightened out the wings to level, flew as close to the
left side of the clouds as possible, and then tried a
fast sharp turn to the right. About halfway through
the turn I saw that if I continued turning I would be
into the clouds before completing the turn. Again
I straightened my wings to level flight and flew
even farther into the funnel.

Looking ahead, I saw what looked like a sinkhole in the valley of our oval path and hoped like
hell there would be a way down out of those jaws
of doom. I felt like a mouse walking across the trig-
ger on a giant rat trap, but I had no choice but to
keep walking and hoping. Our whole world was
closing in on us and all we could do was wait and
wait and hope that the Great Spirit would be with
us just one more time. I felt almost embarrassed to
ask her again. But I did.

The closer we got to the sinkhole the more I
began to realize that it just might be large enough
to spiral down through if I could see the ground
below. Had we actually escaped again, or was
this just another sucker-hole? I kept my fingers

crossed and forced myself to breathe as my heart started to pound again.

About a mile or so farther into the funnel I could start to see patches of earth below, but not quite enough to spiral down through yet. Then I saw that the other side of the sinkhole was a solid wall of darker clouds. I waited another few seconds and looked down again. Still not enough earth below to start a descending turn. Another ten seconds later and I found myself located in what I estimated to be about the middle of the hole. Looking over the sides of the cockpit I thought I could see the outline of the green earth below through a thin layer of clouds. Was I dreaming or had I actually found a way down? I had to make a split-second decision: either start a spiraling turn down through the unknown, or just accept my hopeless situation and fly farther into the funnel and hope for the best. I chose to start the descending turn.

I pulled the throttle back to idle, to slow down, and when we were at seventy miles per hour I started adding right rudder, and the plane began its descent earthward. As the nose dropped I could start to see flashes of green earth through the cloud layers. I was committed at that point to an unknown fate; there would be no turning back.

I knew that the biggest problem in a spiraling turn would be keeping the speed constant and the nose of the plane turning in a circle instead of diving straight down. Unable to see either the horizon or the ground as reference points, all I could do was hold on and hope for the best. Around and around for what seemed like forever, I kept losing altitude and looking for the ground through the smoky clouds. First 7000 feet, then 6500 feet, 6000—we were headed down too fast. "Watch your airspeed, Russ!" I yelled, and added a little left rudder to slow it back down again. "Not too much, you'll stop turning if you over-control!" In and out of the clouds of the sinkhole we went like drunken sailors in the narrow streets of Hong Kong. "What a mess, you idiot, you've finally pushed those limits too far this time."

Down and down, around and around we went like water in a slow-swirling toilet bowl. First 5500 feet, 5000, 4500…4000…but our airspeed seemed to be holding constant. I searched over the sides of the plane for the ground without success. The last thing I needed to see over the nose was a white blanket of clouds below. We were reaching the bottom of the sinkhole.

Then about a thousand feet above the blanket we broke through the clouds. I kicked in left rudder to straighten the wings and pulled back on the stick and leveled out. We were straight and level once more, but inside two layers of another cloud formation—again. For the moment it felt great to just not be spiraling down through the unknown. However, I knew we weren't quite out of the woods yet. We were still flying over a solid overcast area, and with only one handheld radio. But on the horizon I could see the beginning of light blue sky ahead. We had no choice but to "Stay with the plan."

By the time I crossed over the Potomac River, just north of the Dahlgren, Virginia, restricted area, the overcast clouds gradually began opening up and I could see occasional patches of beautiful green earth below. I started breathing a little easier and my heartbeat finally began to slow down. I began to feel that with any luck at all we might just survive the whole ordeal.

I'm thoroughly convinced that both Mother Nature and the Great Spirit have wicked senses of humor. And they both love to mess with me from time to time.

We were treading on dangerous sky, but we envied no earth-bound human as we slowly glided aloft in quiet solitude, suspended over a white layer of clouds like new-fallen snow. Drifting along and looking down at the bed of white silken clouds, I gradually began to relax. A serene peacefulness soon emerged, and we acknowledged that true relief for our stress-beleaguered souls was found only when we ventured aloft and soared with the eagles and hawks. We were truly at one with Mother Nature again.

# CHAPTER 76

**WHEN WE CROSSED** the Patuxent River, I knew we could get down through the broken cloud layer anytime. Shortly thereafter, I was over the Chesapeake Bay, looking down at the water through scattered cumulous clouds. I did a time check and found that I was still flying with at least 50 mph tail winds. Finally, decent tail winds!

From eight thousand feet I looked down at the deep, calm water of the Bay, and then I cast an evil eye upon that damn GPS and thought aloud, "You worthless piece of shit, I'm gonna deep-six your useless ass in the bay right now." But, no matter how hard I pulled and strained against the large tie-down wraps, it wouldn't budge from the metal plate attached to the cockpit frame. I promised myself that it would be the first thing I removed when I got on the ground and inside the hanger. I planned to give it a decent burial right after I beat it to death with a sledgehammer. A good GPS is a marvelous piece of navigation equipment. But outdated, intermittent units will slowly but surely kill you if they get a chance.

After crossing James Island on the Eastern Shore of Maryland, I started a gradual descent towards the Cambridge Airport. The lower I descended, the warmer the sun and temperature became; it was a beautiful summer day with just a few puffy clouds hanging around to welcome us back home again. I called the Cambridge Airport on the radio and found that it was eighty degrees on the ground and that the winds were light and favoring a landing to the southeast on Runway 16. Snap Johnson, at the airport, came back on the radio to welcome me home and then asked if I would need fuel after landing. I told him the only fuel I needed today came in the form of a six-pack, and then all I really wanted was a lawn chair and a maybe a couple of hours to enjoy myself. He laughed.

Slowly reducing the power, I descended towards the airport until I was on final approach. Realizing that I was higher than normal for a short landing, I pulled the throttle back to idle, and with right rudder and left aileron began a slow steep sideslip towards the threshold of the runway.

An almost silent wind gently whispered inside the cockpit. Then, from somewhere off in the distance, I heard a single faint sound that gradually increased in pitch until it was joined by another one, and then they combined with another sound that harmonized into one single musical chord. After three thousand miles of flying, I had just heard the gentle singing of the wires for the third time.

# CHAPTER 77

**AFTER TOUCHDOWN, I** checked my watch and realized that, even with all the radio problems, I had flown the last 165 miles in only 55 minutes. That works out to be a whopping 179 mph over-all, not too shabby for a fifty-year-old biplane. The wind gods and Mother Nature had finally smiled down on us.

A few people were waving out in front of the maintenance shop and airport terminal as I taxied to the hanger. It felt good to be home again. A couple of friends helped me put the plane away, and I gave them a condensed version of the trip and promised to share more with them later. These great and special flying friends of mine understood how tired I was and gave me the space I needed to recuperate.

Then I called my soul mate and asked her, "Have you got a cold beer for a tired cowboy?" For years this had been my way of letting her know that I was high, dry, and safe at the airport. She said, "You bet, be there within the hour."

Before placing the cockpit cover over the windshields, I removed the GPS and went looking for the biggest hammer I could find. But my anger had long since passed, and the memory of how it had saved my butt not more than twenty-four hours earlier became clearer in my mind. So, instead of destroying it, I suspended it above my workbench with lacing wire as a reminder that if I was going to fly using GPS, I needed to buy an updated model.

The late model Toyota Tundra pickup truck was still parked beside the end of the hangers. We were back in the same time zone—as expected. Maybe the 50 mph tailwind had pushed us forward the additional fifteen years. Or was it the extra four times I had wound the clock at Eagles Nest?

# CHAPTER 78

**WHILE WAITING ON** my ride home, I sat in a lawn chair in front of the plane with the hanger door open. A small flock of sea gulls were soaring along overhead on the soft summer breeze and several meadowlarks were singing in the distance as I closed my eyes and felt the sun on my face, and thought back on the trip in its entirety. I'd had a few obstacles and problems along the way, but nothing so severe that it would keep me from taking the same trip again. I'd do it all over again in a heartbeat. I think all true barnstormers would feel the same way. I'd learned a few (hard) lessons, and I'd polished up some basic navigation skills needed for good basic VFR flying again. It was, indeed, a great trip, and one that I will never forget in this lifetime.

I still wasn't sure why John Grace came to me in the dream and led me through the trip. And I still don't think there was just one reason why he

was there. There were several significant and posi-
tive things that happened to me on the trip. I think
John was trying to let me know that dreams are
real, and life is short, at best; and we need to follow our dreams and live life to the fullest on a daily
basis.

It had been great to break away from my routine and go back in time barnstorming again,
if only for nine days. And it was nice to see the
American spirit still alive in St. Francis and elsewhere. But I think the greatest thing that happened on the trip was finding peace again with
my oldest daughter. Thank you, John.

# EPILOGUE

We finally sold Jackie's Cub, but we found an even better one and we're enjoying it more now than ever. We're still arguing politics, religion, and flying, but in a more civilized manner. Guess we'll always have our differences of opinion, but that's a good thing.

Mel is starting to take flying lessons in the Cub, so it's probably only a matter of time until I have to wait in line to fly and go sightseeing along the rivers. Oh well, females outnumber me at home, so why should it be any different at the airport? I just can't win.

At this point we're planning a return-barnstorming trip to St. Francis next June, if all goes well. Maybe it will be a combined Cub-and-Stearman kind of trip. Sounds like a plan to me. I'll keep you posted.

**RUSS WILDER** is a retired Homeland Security planner and a commercial pilot with over 20 years flying experience as a barnstorming pilot. Along with his love for flying old biplanes and restoring antique aircraft, he has flown over 5000 hours across America as a charter pilot, air show pilot, flight instructor, spray pilot, and banner pilot. He lives on a small farm in Maryland with his wife and daughter.